ATTACKE...

Because of your computer skills and your familiarity with the planet, you have been selected to accompany Brim Darkstar and his crack Unit Five team of troubleshooters to the planet New Pale in an effort to discover why all communication has been cut off with the Frontier's most important supplier of food.

Landing in a field, you are about to begin your investigation of the planet when suddenly a gigantic machine, with rows of sharp spikes on its front, begins to crash through the field toward you! You realize the spikes of the harvester agbot could grind you to fodder in seconds if you don't do something immediately.

What will you do?

1) If you want to try to stop the agbot by attempting to get to its manual controls, turn to page 116.

2) If you choose to try to stop the agbot by shooting it with your laser gun, turn to page 146.

3) But if you want to run for your space craft and try to get away, turn to page 10.

Whatever choice you make, you are sure to find adventure as you seek to unravel
the secret of the
CAPTIVE PLANET

An ENDLESS QUEST® Book   #17

CAPTIVE PLANET

BY MORRIS SIMON

A STAR FRONTIERS™ ADVENTURE BOOK

Cover Art by Clyde Caldwell
Interior Art by Sam Grainger

TSR, Inc.

To Andy

CAPTIVE PLANET
© Copyright 1984, TSR, Inc.
All Rights Reserved.

Distributed to the book trade in the United States by Random House, Inc., and in Canada by Random House of Canada, Ltd.

Distributed in the United Kingdom by TSR (UK) Ltd. Distributed to the toy and hobby trade by regional distributors.

DUNGEONS & DRAGONS, STAR FRONTIERS, and PICK A PATH TO ADVENTURE are trademarks owned by TSR, Inc.

D&D and ENDLESS QUEST are registered trademarks owned by TSR, Inc.

First printing: July, 1984
Printed in the United States of America
Library of Congress Catalog Card Number: 84-50718
ISBN: 0-88038-078-0

9 8 7 6 5 4 3 2 1

TSR, Inc.
P.O. Box 756
Lake Geneva, WI 53147

TSR (UK), Ltd.
The Mill, Rathmore Road
Cambridge CB1 4AD
United Kingdom

ou are about to set off on an adventure in which YOU will meet many dangers — and face many decisions. YOUR choices will determine how the story turns out. So be careful . . . you must choose wisely!

Do not read this book from beginning to end! Instead, as you are faced with a decision, follow the instructions and keep turning to the pages where your choices lead you until you come to an end. At any point, YOUR choice could bring success — or disaster!

You can read CAPTIVE PLANET many times, with many different results, so if you make an unwise choice, go back to the beginning and start again!

Good luck on YOUR adventure!

In this story, you are Andru, a talented young computer student. You have recently been sent by your scientist parents from your native planet, New Pale, to study at the highly respected Computer Institute on Gran Quivera. As the story begins, you are grappling with a particularly challenging problem in robotics. . . .

Your fingers tremble as you snip the last thin wire in the robot's brain. You have only twenty-two seconds to attach the last magnetic bypass clip to the hand computer so that you can control the heavy machine! The room about you is deathly quiet, and you know that they are watching you, but you must not let their tense stares make you nervous.

You grab the needle-nosed pliers and reach inside to clip the last circuit. Then you notice the bypass wire isn't long enough! "FOUR-TEEN SECONDS!" your wrist timer flashes. You get another bypass wire from your kit and coolly clip it to the first one, then connect the robot to your computer.

You have no time left to check the circuit. You press the START button and freeze, expecting to hear the alarm. A string of flashing zeroes on your wrist timer tells you that your time is gone! Suddenly the robot's photo-cell eyes flash to life.

"I am now programmed to report a success-ful bypass," it says in a flat, metallic voice. For a moment, the room is silent. Then everyone begins to cheer.

"You did it, Dru!" "Way to go, boy!" "You can work on my robots anytime, Clayton!"

"That's enough," interrupts the silver-haired woman standing beside you at the front of the classroom. "I have something to say before the period ends. Turn it off, Dru, and return to your seat."

You nod and push the power switch. The

robot janitor's photocells blink off, and you return to your desk.

"Computer Specialist Clayton has just passed his first examination in robotics," the teacher announces, "but only in a very risky way. What was your mistake, Dru?"

"I didn't test the circuits," you answer quickly. "I just didn't have time."

"That's correct, Dru. That was merely a vacuum cleaner. If it had been something more dangerous, you might have blown up the entire Computer Institute and most of Port Loren along with it! But it was a fine job," she adds, her voice softening, "especially for someone so young. Keep up the good work, and you'll be the first fifteen-year-old at the institute with both computer and robotics skills. Class dismissed!"

Your teacher's praise makes you feel good about the long hours of study you've spent at Corporation's Computer Institute on Gran Quivera, the capital planet of the United Planetary Federation.

Your parents are scientists working for the Pan-Galactic Corporation, the largest private company in the Federation, with colonies nearly everywhere in the explored sectors of the Frontier. Ever since your early childhood in the agricultural colony of New Pale, at the outer fringe of the Frontier, you've been playing with computers and robots. The Corporation invited you to the institute for advanced training when you were only twelve, and already you are studying Level 3 computers.

As you gather the tools of your portable tool kit, called a robcomkit, several friends ask you to go with them to the game room.

"Maybe later," you reply. "I'm scheduled for another call to my parents on New Pale in ten minutes." Only a month ago, you left your home planet in the Truane's Star system to return to school. Since then, each call you have placed to your parents has been interrupted by a strange noise. You're starting to worry a little about your parents, isolated on a sparsely populated world more than eight light years away.

You make your way to the Corporation's Communication Center, located on the top floor of the same building as the institute. Inside, several other Corporation employees and students are using the high-speed communicators, which are capable of sending and receiving messages across the entire Frontier. You find an empty booth and punch the code for your parents' laboratory on New Pale.

The video screen begins to blink. Finally it begins to glow, and the speakers hum smoothly. You know that it's almost noon at the research station on New Pale. Soon the call buzzer will interrupt your parents' lunch, and you'll see their faces on the screen.

The steady hum suddenly stops and is replaced by a loud hissing sound. The orange glow turns to a snowstorm of white dots so bright that you squint. It's the same kind of interference you have seen each time before!

You push a button for assistance, and almost immediately a communications cybot sticks its plasteel head into your booth.

"What is the problem, sir?" asks the machine in its best "programmed-to-help" voice. Quickly you tell it about the static.

"Perhaps this communicator is defective, sir," says the cybot in its peculiar flat tone. It pushes a special maintenance code, and a series of numbers flash on the screen. You know that the two machines are talking to each other, but their language is too advanced for you to understand.

"This is highly unusual," says the puzzled cybot. "The circuit is perfect all the way to the Truane's Star sector. It is broken only at New Pale. I fear this problem is beyond my level, sir. Perhaps you should wait a week to see if the static will clear, or you could report it to Star Law. It may be a security problem."

Hoping that nothing has happened to your parents, you leave the Communication Center and try to decide what to do.

1) If you decide to report the problem to Star Law, turn to page 13.

2) If you would rather seek advice before you decide, turn to page 22.

3) Or if you choose to wait another week, as the cybot suggested, turn to page 39.

"We can't stop a harvester!" you shout. "Head for the ship! It's our only chance!"

You run through the rows of mannakan toward the scouter, with Skitsi and Kit right behind you. Jan tries to get Seel to move faster, but the Dralasite is hobbling as fast as a blob can run, trying in panic to grow several more legs. Darkstar and Erl draw their weapons and back quickly toward the ship.

The giant agbot crashes through the mannakan and pauses several hundred meters away to scan the field with its photoeyes. As soon as they focus on the scouter, the harvester rumbles at full speed toward the little starship.

Everyone except Darkstar and Erl are inside by the time you hear the roar of its treads. The two fighters aim their laser and gyrojet weapons at the agbot's control cabin and start blasting. You see bright sparks fill the air as the huge machine thunders to a stop only a few meters from the ship.

"Let's see if we can find out why that thing went crazy!" shouts Erl.

Jan and Seel start down the ramp toward the disabled machine, with you right behind them. Suddenly the Dralasite stops and looks at his toxyrad gauge.

"Radiation!" he shouts. "Theta rays are leaking from the agbot!"

"We must have damaged the reactor!" yells Brim. "Quick, everybody, into the ship!"

It only takes seconds for everyone to get back inside and close the hatch. Skitsi imme-

diately starts the engines, and Jan hits the antigrav switch. You feel the scouter start to float upward just as a bright fireball seems to envelop it. In the instant of consciousness before the heat of the blast melts the scouter, you realize that the agbot's nuclear reactor has exploded, and your adventure has come to a tragic . . .

END

Inside the elevator, you decide to report the mysterious static to Star Law. As the police of the Federation, the Star Law Rangers have outposts throughout the Frontier. Perhaps they'll be able to tell you if anything unusual has happened to the colony on New Pale.

Star Law Headquarters is in Port Loren, not far from the Pan-Galactic Corporation building where you live and go to school. Inside, you see a Dralasite "blob" wearing a Ranger corporal's hat. Her two eyespots throb as they study your Corporation uniform.

"What can we do for a young Corporation student with such a worried look?" she asks in a motherly voice that makes you want to tell her everything. You know Dralasites are excellent interrogators because of their special talents in personal conversation.

"I need to see someone about my parents. I've tried to call them six times in the past two weeks, but I can't get through!"

"Relax," the corporal says soothingly. "Give me your identity card and start from the beginning." While she codes your name into her desk computer, you describe the strange signals that keep interrupting your calls.

"New Pale, you say?" the Dralasite asks suddenly, her eyespots brightening against her wrinkled gray skin. "How long has it been since you were on New Pale, Dru?"

"Only a month. I returned to Port Loren for the new term at the Computer Institute as soon as our vacation was over."

"Just a moment," she says quickly. "We might have some information for you!" You watch her three hands fly over the buttons of her keyboard. Then she flashes you a Drala-site version of a smile. "Someone will help you in just a few moments, Dru," she says. Soon you hear the hollow sound of footsteps in the empty corridor. A small, wiry Ranger captain, not much taller than you, comes around a corner and offers you a friendly handshake.

"Computer Specialist Andru Clayton from New Pale?" he asks, shaking your hand firmly.

"Yes, I'm Dru Clayton," you reply.

"I'm Captain Tyson, Dru. I may have some news for you. Let's go someplace where we can talk about this more comfortably." You follow the Ranger to a small room furnished with only two chairs and a table. You sit across the table from the officer and wait expectantly for him to begin.

"Now, Dru," he says seriously, "exactly when did you leave New Pale?"

"A month ago!" you exclaim, beginning to feel irritated. "That's what I just told the corporal! Has anything happened to my parents?"

"I'll ask the questions, Dru!" the captain says firmly. "This is a Federation matter now. Just answer my questions if you want to help your parents!" Tyson's strong manner confuses you. Something very strange must be happening on New Pale, and your parents are somehow involved! "Once more," begins Tyson, "exactly when did you leave New Pale?"

"EXACTLY twenty-seven standard days ago!" you answer angrily. Both New Pale and Galactic Standard days are twenty hours long, so you don't need to calculate the date.

"And you've had no contact with New Pale since that time?" Tyson asks insistently.

"That's why I'm here!" you cry, feeling frustrated. "I haven't been able to get through to my parents, and I want to know why! I came here for help, but all I've gotten so far are questions! What's happening on New Pale?" The Ranger stares at you for a few seconds as if he's trying to decide if you're lying. Then he tries to calm you.

"Settle down, Dru," he says. "We've had some very serious reports about New Pale, and we're still investigating them. I'll tell you what we know if you'll promise to help us and if you'll agree not to discuss this matter with anyone else!"

You begin to realize that things are more serious than you imagined. You wonder if you did the right thing in coming to Star Law.

1) If you decide to help the Rangers and not discuss New Pale with anyone else, turn to page 88.

2) But if you decide that you've made a mistake and want to ask someone else for help, turn to page 114.

"Are you Computer Specialist Andru Clayton?"

The security cybot had bypassed your thumb-sealed door, which means that it's Level 4 or higher. You stare at the glassy photoeyes, knowing that someone important must be watching your reaction.

"Yes, I'm Dru Clayton," you say sleepily.

"Please follow me to the dean's office immediately, CompSpec Dru," says the cybot. "I have been programmed to tell you that the matter concerns your parents on New Pale."

"Well, why didn't you say so?" you say. You follow the cybot through the silent metal corridor to Dean Luxtar's office in the administrative wing.

The shiny blue door panel slides open with a soft whoosh, revealing a room with a large synwood desk. Luxtar's dull green shell gleams in the lighted room as he focuses his dark Vrusk eyes on you.

"Come in, Dru—and shut the door," he clicks. The Dean's eight legs are hidden behind the heavy desk, but the fierce mandibles and waving antennae still remind you of a giant grasshopper.

"Have a seat, Dru, and listen to this recording from the last Star Law shuttle that tried to land on New Pale," the Vrusk buzzes, pressing a button on his desk. The sound of crackling static fills the office. Then the voice of some unknown Star Law Ranger breaks through the noise.

"We can see the mannakan fields," says the voice. "They seem quiet—too quiet!"

"Lieutenant!" yells a second voice. "The controls are locked! I . . . can't . . . seem to—"

"UP!" screams the first voice. "Watch out for—"

A high-pitched hum suddenly replaces the voices, then stops, leaving only the steady crackling sound. It is the same static you've heard when you tried to call your parents!

Dean Luxtar flicks off the speakers. "New Pale has been quiet for more than a month, Dru!" he says in his strange Vruskan clicking speech. "We don't know what's happened on the planet. No one has been able to even communicate with New Pale, let alone land there."

"A month! But—but that's when I left!" you cry.

"Yes, Dru, I know," Luxtar buzzes slowly. "It now appears that you were very likely the last person to leave the planet! As for your parents, or anyone else on New Pale, we simply don't know what has happened to them!"

"But the Corporation merchants visit New Pale every three days for a load of mannakan! The whole Frontier depends upon that crop!"

"That's exactly right, Dru," says a deep voice from behind you.

Whirling around, you see a tall, muscular human standing next to another Vrusk. The man is clad in a tight blue skeinsuit and is smiling beneath a dark moustache. His com-

panion is studying you carefully with his antennae.

"I'm Brim Darkstar," says the handsome man, "and this overgrown locust is my chief scientist, Skitsi Dzig. We need to talk to you, Dru."

"THE Brim Darkstar?" you exclaim. You've read so much about the legendary adventurer that you hardly believe he really exists.

"Well, Dru, I've never met anyone else named after a black hole," he jokes, "so I guess I'm the one you mean." You've read that a Ranger named him "Darkstar" after his unknown parents and their entire colony were swallowed in a black hole. Brim was found adrift in deep space, a baby in a tiny escape capsule, the sole survivor of the worst starship disaster in Frontier history!

"Wh—why do you need to talk to me, Mr. Darkstar?" you stammer, amazed to be face-to-face with the greatest of your childhood heroes.

"Call me 'Brim,' " he says with a friendly smile. "We need your help because you were the last person to leave New Pale. We must learn all we can about your home colony before we leave for the Truane sector."

"Did you say 'we'? Do you mean Unit Five?" you ask excitedly. The famous team of adventurers and agents for the Corporation are also legends. Brim Darkstar's Unit Five has explored more sectors of deep space for colonization than any other technical research team in the Frontier! You've read thrilling tales of their battles against terrible monsters—the firedragons of Yast, the giant slithers created by the strange worm-people called Sathar. . . .

"Yes, Dru," replies Brim, "Unit Five's going to New Pale, and in a matter of hours! We know from what you've told Dean Luxtar, and from our own sources inside the Federation, that Star Law is launching a fleet of starships to battle the unknown forces that are controlling your colony. We must get there first and solve that problem, or the invasion could destroy the mannakan fields!"

"The Corporation places the greatest value upon the mannakan fields of New Pale!" clicks Skitsi Dzig, his antennae quivering animatedly. "The entire Federation depends upon the mannakan from your planet!"

"All of our maps are too old," says Brim Darkstar. "The merchant ships get only as far as the Truane City starport, and their crews can't tell us anything about the rest of the planet. As far as we know, you're the only person outside of New Pale who can give us enough current data to plan our mission."

"Dru, I want you to tell these gentlemen everything you can remember about the colony just before you left," buzzes Dean Luxtar.

"We may require more than that," adds Brim seriously. "We need a guide along, in case we can't land at the starport. I've read your file, Dru. It says that you worked with your parents in the mannakan fields."

"Yes," clicks Skitsi Dzig, "and Dean Luxtar tells me that you've already mastered Level Three programs, even though you're only fifteen years old."

"Dru came to us from New Pale when he was twelve," says Luxtar. "His parents are pioneer technicians in the colony. They've been teaching Dru computer skills ever since his childhood."

"Plus hunting skills!" you add. "My dad and I have hunted with laser rifles in every forest on New Pale."

"Excellent!" exclaims Brim. "Skitsi, it seems that we have a new recruit for Unit Five. And he can shoot as well as run computers! Now, if Dean Luxtar will only let us borrow his star student for a few weeks. . . ."

"I have no objection," says Luxtar. "Dru is far ahead on his homework. But you really need to ask him. He may prefer to wait to see if his parents can get a message through."

You pause as all eyes turn to you, and you know that they are waiting for your decision.

1) If you want to join Unit Five on its mission to New Pale, turn to page 57.

2) But if you want to remain at school until you receive further information, turn to page 26.

You're much too concerned about your parents to wait another week. You also know that the Pan-Galactic Corporation likes to handle its own business without involving the Federation's Star Law police, and New Pale is a private Corporation colony. By the time the elevator reaches the floor of the Computer Institute, you've decided to ask the dean's advice. As a Corporation officer, he may be able to help you.

Dean Luxtar's secretary tells you that he's out of the office. You leave your name and a video message describing your problems with the calls, and the secretary assures that the dean will see it as soon as he returns.

When you get to your room, you try to study, but your thoughts are too troubled. After several hours, you fall into an exhausted sleep. In your dreams, you try to warn your parents of some unknown danger, but they don't seem to hear you. You hear a strange voice calling your name, louder and louder, until you wake with a start. You sit up suddenly and find yourself staring into the blank face of a large cybot leaning over your bed!

Please turn to page 16.

"I say we've got to stick together," you tell Jan. "We'd have a better chance then to fight whatever the Brain sends our way. It means a postponement of our mission, but at least we'll get another chance."

"You may have a point, Dru," says Jan, "but let's do something before the Brain finds us!"

"The first thing we have to do is get off this archway," says Darkstar. "It'd be easy to trap us here in the middle with nowhere to go but down!"

"I'm afraid we'll have to stay here until Skitsi is able to be moved," says Seel. "Even if we could carry him, it might be dangerous in his condition."

Brim frowns and glances toward both ends of the bridge. "Do what you can for him, Seel. We'd better post some guards at both ends of this bridge before we're sealed off!"

"It might be too late for that, Brim!" exclaims Jan. "I hear something coming down the walkway to the right!"

Everyone freezes as they notice the sound of some kind of vehicle coming from the direction of the mushroom shaft where you entered the tunnel.

In the distance, along the wall, you see a small hovercycle speeding toward the archway. It's armed with some sort of large weapon and has two security cybots riding in it.

"It's a sonic devastator!" Erl exclaims. "We don't have a chance against that thing!"

"We have to get Skitsi off the bridge to the

other side!" says Brim. All of you except Jan begin to drag the Vrusk's heavy body across the archway. The hovercycle stops at the end of the bridge, and the two cybots train the devastator on you.

"HALT!" booms a deep voice from a speaker on the vehicle. "YOU HAVE ENTERED A RESTRICTED ZONE! IF YOU DO NOT HALT, WE WILL FIRE UPON YOU!"

You all try to drag Skitsi's body faster, but Seel makes you slow down. "If you jar him any more, he'll be dead by the time we get to the other side!" cautious the Dralasite medic.

Suddenly you hear a whine from across the tunnel.

"Get down!" Erl yells. "They're firing!"

Before you can do as he says, a wave of sound deafens you and knocks you to the walkway. You can see Brim saying something to you, but you can't make out his words. Your bones are vibrating so fast that you feel the heat building inside.

When the second blast hits, the last thing you see are the trembling bodies of your friends as you realize that this is . . .

THE END

"Mr. Darkstar, I'd like to go with you, but I can't!" you say after a few seconds. "I'm the only one left who knows anything about the colony. If I stay here, I can guide Star Law if anything happens to you!"

The famed explorer studies you for a moment, then pats your shoulder. "That's a brave decision, Dru," he says. "I know how badly you want to help your parents. If you'll just tell us everything you can about the colony, we can update the maps in our computer."

Skitsi Dzig pulls a small telecorder from his belt. For more than two hours, you answer every question the two explorers ask you.

"I think that'll do," Brim says finally. "Now we can go to New Pale with a fighting chance. I wish that you were coming with us, Dru, but I'm glad someone will be around to lead Star Law to the colony if we fail."

"I just hope it helps!" you exclaim. "Please let me know what's happening."

"We will, Dru," Brim promises. "Give us two weeks before you go to Star Law with it."

You wait anxiously for word and ask Dean Luxtar about Unit Five almost every day during the following two weeks. Finally the kindly Vrusk calls you to his office. As soon as you enter, you sense that something's wrong.

"I'm afraid the news about Unit Five isn't good, Dru!" clicks Luxtar. "We lost communication with them just as they were landing on New Pale, and we think the same thing happened to the Ranger ships!"

"I've got to go to Star Law Headquarters, Dean Luxtar!" you exclaim. "I promised Brim Darkstar that I'd lead a rescue mission if anything like this happened!"

"I'm sorry, Dru," he clicks, "but that's impossible. Star Law has declared New Pale off limits until a military expedition can investigate. This has a lot of top people in both the Corporation and the Federation scared. Unit Five was our best team of trouble-shooters!"

"But they need to talk to me first!" you cry. "Darkstar and Skitsi Dzig wanted me to guide the Rangers to New Pale!"

"I'm afraid that's out of the question now, Dru," says Luxtar. "Star Law has classified this operation a top secret military mission, closed to all civilians."

"What are they going to do?" you ask. "My parents may be in danger, along with Unit Five and the whole colony!"

The wise old Vrusk chops the air with his mandibles. "That depends on Star Law," he buzzes. "Maybe tomorrow, maybe never! All we can do is wait. It's out of our hands now."

Suddenly you wish that you had gone to New Pale with Brim Darkstar and his crew. Now the only thing you can do is hope that your father and mother are safe and that the brave team of Unit Five is still able to find them.

THE END

The roof of the Computer Center is closer than the street, but the cybodragons might be on top of you if you land there. Looking at the narrow space between the Computer Center and the Security Center, you decide to land the copter on the street. The cybodragons might not be able to follow the vehicle in such a cramped space.

"Hold on!" you yell. "I'm landing in the street!"

"Good!" says Erl. "Maybe we can get through to the Brain Room after all!" The Yazirian pulls his sonic sword from its scabbard and stands poised in the open hatch of the copter.

"Brim's all right!" yells Jan as Seel injects Darkstar with some stimdose. The handsome leader begins to stir almost instantly.

Suddenly you feel a wave of sound shake the copter. Someone is firing at you with a sonic weapon of some kind! You see a single cybot standing in the street below, aiming a disruptor at you. Without waiting for you to land, Erl screams his fierce Yazirian battle cry and leaps from the hatch!

It is the first time you have ever seen a Yazirian use his skinwings. To you, Erl looks like a giant squird as he soars gracefully toward the cybot. He lands lightly on his bare feet behind the humanoid and charges it with his sonic sword upraised.

The Yazirian is a blur of golden fur and swirling scarlet cape as he slashes at the cybot

with his invisible blade. In an instant, the humanoid is lying on the pavement sputtering electrical fire.

Suddenly you see a heavy beam of red light from the Security Center. It drills a fiery hole in the pavement between Erl's hairy feet. The warrior glances up quickly at you and starts running for an alley between two buildings. Just as his cloak clears the corner, another laser beam blasts a chunk of concrete from the building.

From the corner of your eye, you see more armed cybots spilling into the street from the Security Center. "Get ready to run for cover!" you tell everyone as the copter hits the pavement.

Skitsi already has the hatch open and jumps to the street, followed by Kit and the others. You switch off the engine and leap from the damaged copter onto the hard pavement.

Please turn to page 66.

"From what I've seen, the problem must have something to do with the main computer in Truane City," you suggest to Brim. "Everything on New Pale is controlled by it, even the starport and communication systems. That's where we need to start."

"That sounds right," says Brim. "This whole business could be just one colossal computer error."

"But how will we land?" asks Jan. "Unless we turn our landing systems over to the main computer in Truane City, starport security will shoot us down!"

"Not if we land on the outskirts of the city," says Darkstar. "We've got a radar screen, and our antigrav will let us land anywhere we choose."

"And once we're on the ground, we can handle any security cybots they send," adds Erl.

"For once, I agree with you, Ch'oth Erl," clicks Skitsi, his antennae twitching excitedly.

"That's it, then," says Brim. "We'll try the city first."

As you approach Truane City, the computer locates a level spot on a field near the starport. You recognize it as a park where you've played soccer with your friends. Jan's skilled hands operate the antigrav device. The scouter slows to a stop in midair, then begins to float downward as lightly as a feather.

Suddenly, Brim leaps up from his control panel to look at the viewer. "We're being controlled from the ground!" he yells. "Something is interfering with the antigrav!"

The scouter jerks violently and begins to plummet toward the surface of your home planet! The sudden burst of speed throws you against the wall. Just before you lose consciousness, you see the grassy field loom large beneath you, and you realize that someone else will have to discover the mysterious forces that have taken over the fields of New Pale.

THE END

The elevator doors slide open silently on the eighth floor, and the four of you enter a long, well-lit corridor. There are numerous doors on both sides of the hall, but they have no markings of any kind.

"Does this look familiar, Dru?" asks Brim.

"No," you reply, confused. "I've never been in this part of the Computer Center."

"See if Kit can tell us which of these doors leads to the Brain Room," suggests Brim.

"That data is not in my memory, Master Dru," says Kit when you ask it. "The map only identifies the eighth floor as the location."

Toward the end of the passage, you see a familiar-looking green box on the wall. "Brim, I think that's a computer terminal!"

The four of you move silently to the panel. The green box proves to be a terminal used by maintenance and security robots to get instructions about their duties.

"Maybe we could just plug Kit into it and find out where the Brain is!" says Erl.

"That might be dangerous," says Brim. "If the Brain links with Kit, it might have control of our only computer. What do you think, Dru?"

1) If you want to plug Kit into the terminal to try to locate the Brain, turn to page 52.

2) If would rather keep looking for the Brain on your own, turn to page 128.

"The only way I've ever entered the Computer Center is through the front door," you tell the others.

"I'm sure the Brain will have the street guarded," says Brim, "but perhaps we can fight our way into the building. We have weapons, and maybe Packy can provide more help."

Your friend shakes his head. "We only have a handful of troops to stop anything the Brain sends our way. The best I can do is supply you with a sonic devastator for the ground car."

"We'll take it!" Erl growls fiercely. "I once held off a warbot with one of those things!"

"You may have to again!" says Packy. "We believe there's a warbot at the Security Center. You might be able to stop it with the devastator if you hit it just right."

"How does a sonic devastator work?" you ask.

"It's just like a sonic disruptor, only much more powerful," Packy explains. "They both generate a powerful beam of sound that causes the molecules of a target to vibrate so fast that they they heat up until the target disintegrates!"

"Well, what are we waiting for?" Erl exclaims. "Let's go pull the Brain's plug!"

Within twenty minutes, you're speeding toward Truane City in Station Alpha's largest ground car. Erl has installed the sonic devastator atop the large vehicle and rides behind it, grinning into the wind, his dark goggles gleaming in the sunlight.

Inside the ground car, you help Skitsi and Kit study the city map while Jan and Seel keep their eyes peeled for anything unusual. Brim handles the manual controls as if the heavy vehicle were a light sports skimmer.

In the distant haze, you spot the first buildings on the fringe of Truane City. Brim sees them, too, and tells Skitsi to plot their position on the map.

"Do you recognize those buildings, Dru?" the Vrusk asks.

"Yes," you say excitedly, pointing at the map. "We're coming in from the southeast, right here by the Entertainment Center."

"Do you think the Brain knows we're coming?" Seel asks nervously.

"I'm sure it does," clicks Skitsi. "We passed three agbots in a field a while ago, and I saw their photoeyes following us."

A quiver of excitement ripples through the Dralasite's shapeless body, and his gray protoplasm darkens to a bluish shade.

"What's the quickest way to the Computer Center?" calls Brim from the pilot's seat.

"Bear to the right at the Entertainment Center," you reply. "There's a skimmer track that leads straight to the Security Center. We'll have to go around it to get to the Computer Center."

You watch the streets carefully as the ground car rumbles past the familiar buildings. Skimmers are parked along the track, but none are moving. You see the Security

Center just ahead, but there is no sign of life anywhere.

As Brim guides the heavy ground car around the tall Security Center, you suddenly see something that makes you break out in a cold sweat. Straight ahead of you, in the middle of the widest street in Truane City, is one of the largest machines you've ever seen!

"The warbot!" Erl hollers from above. The huge war machine, three times the size of your ground car, is blocking the entire street. You'll have to go around it to get to the Computer Center!

Erl fires the sonic devastator, and you hear a matching blast from the warbot. The sound is so intense that the air vibrates, surrounding the warbot with layers of shimmering light. All of a sudden, the humming stops, silenced by a thick sonic screen shielding the warbot from the devastator.

Jan yells something, but you can't hear a word she's saying. The sonic screen absorbs all sound, so that you hear nothing at all. Brim backs the ground car away from the screen, and the first sound you hear is Skitsi's buzzing voice.

"Those agbots must have spotted the devastator!" he says. "The Brain had the warbot ready with that sonic screen!"

There is a sudden glare of blinding light and the smell of burning metal as a laser beam strikes the ground car. A shower of sparks covers the front of the vehicle.

"It's a laser cannon!" yells Brim. "That war-bot has more firepower than our scouter! We can't move! Everybody get out of here!"

Ch'oth Erl has already leaped from the top of the car, using his wings of thin skin to sail lightly to the street. Through the dense smoke, you see the agile Yazirian dart between some buildings, holding his sonic sword upraised.

In panic, everyone scrambles out of the burning ground car onto the paved street. Your eyes are blinded by the smoke. When they begin to clear, you see a whole squad of security cybots closing in on you!

Please turn to page 66.

As the elevator takes you back down to the level of the Computer Institute, the thought of asking Star Law to investigate the problem seems silly to you. You can imagine what the Rangers would say:

"Just some interstellar noise, boy! Nothing to worry about. After all, New Pale's more than eight light years away. It might take months to get through!"

You begin to laugh at yourself for worrying so much and decide not to mention the matter to anyone at the institute, either. "They'd just say I was a typical homesick student," you think.

During the next several days, you forget about the problem and concentrate on your studies. In the middle of the following week, you try to call New Pale again. When you enter the code for your home planet, the video screen suddenly fills with the seal of the Federation. As you watch, a message flashes on the panel:

"YOUR CALL CANNOT BE PROCESSED. THE UNITED PLANETARY FEDERATION HAS DECLARED THE NEW PALE SECTOR CLOSED TO ALL CIVILIAN COMMUNICATIONS. A MILITARY EMERGENCY EXISTS IN THAT SECTOR. ALL INQUIRIES SHOULD BE DIRECTED TO STAR LAW HEADQUARTERS AT PORT LOREN. END MESSAGE."

The screen darkens, leaving you confused and frightened. You rush into the corridor and take the elevator to the street level. Star Law Headquarters is only a few blocks from the Pan-Galactic building. At the receptionist's desk, a Dralasite "blob" in a Ranger corporal's uniform asks for your identity card and studies it carefully. You tell her about the message you've just read and ask her for more details.

"Please wait a moment. I'll find out whatever I can about the New Pale situation," she says softly, pressing the buttons on her keyboard with her three hands. You wait in tense silence as the Dralasite's twin eyespots study the screen. After a few seconds, she speaks in a firmer voice.

"All information pertaining to New Pale has been classified as secret by the Federation, Dru. I can't tell you anything more about that sector until the security classification is canceled."

Stunned, you leave Star Law Headquarters and return to the institute. Instead of going to your room, you decide to ask Dean Luxtar for advice. As the chief Corporation officer at the institute, he may be able to tell you more, since New Pale is a private Corporation colony.

The middle-aged Vrusk welcomes you into his office and listens to your desperate plea for help. When you've finished, Dean Luxtar chops the air with his gleaming mandibles, something Vrusk do when they're thinking. Finally he tries to console you in his buzzing voice.

"Dru, the only thing I can tell you is that both the Corporation and Star Law have lost many of our best men and ships trying to land on New Pale. We have sent our best teams of experts to investigate the situation, but none have returned."

"What abut my parents and the other colonists? And what about the mannakan crop?" you cry. "Every planet in the Federation depends upon the Corporation's shipments of mannakan!"

"We can only hope it's not too late for either them or the mannakan," Dean Luxtar buzzes. "Until we know more, there's nothing we can do. If we had been alerted sooner, perhaps things would be different."

You return to your room and try to rest, but you keep hearing the dean's last words. You wonder if the situation might have been better if you had reported the communications problem earlier. At least you're safe on Gran Quivera and will be ready to help solve the mystery of New Pale whenever someone gives you the chance. Until then, all you can do is wait—and hope.

THE END

The look on Kit's plasteel face has you worried, but you feel sure that the cybot will be able to protect its memory circuits. You decide to wait and let Kit try to learn more about the voice.

"Ask the voice to identify itself," Skitsi commands his cybot. Kit's photoeyes sweep the cabin, focusing upon each of you briefly.

"AH! THE ONES CALLED UNIT FIVE!" the mysterious voice booms suddenly. "AND THE HUMAN BOY CALLED ANDRU CLAYTON!"

Some unknown force is controlling Kit, using its photoeyes to study all of you! You reach for the plug to disconnect the cybot from the agbot's computer, but a shower of sparks stops you.

"IT IS TOO LATE FOR THAT!" booms the voice again. "I HAVE CONTROL OF BI-ZKIT. THE CYBOT WILL USE ITS ATTACK PROGRAM IF YOU INTERFERE AGAIN!"

"Get out of my way, Dru!" growls Ch'oth Erl, drawing his sonic sword. "I'll switch that tin bug off!"

You hear a high-pitched whining sound as the brave Yazirian swings the sword at the cable connecting Kit to the computer. Just then a thin laser beam darts from Kit's chest, hitting the warrior's arm! The sonic sword flies to the floor with a clatter as the Yazirian howls with pain. Seel hurries to apply some biocort ointment from his medkit to the laser wound.

"I WARNED YOU!" says the voice. "I CAN NOW USE BI-ZKIT TO CONTROL YOUR SHIP'S COMPUTER BY ITS LINK WITH THE CYBOT. WATCH YOUR SCOUTER!"

Through the window of the agbot, you see the scouter slowly begin to lift from the ground. Whatever force is controlling Kit has taken over the antigrav.

"Let's get out of here before we get blasted with our own laser cannons!" yells Brim.

But it's too late. The scouter hovers above the crippled agbot and aims the powerful cannons at it. You know that the harvester's nuclear reactor will explode any second now, and when it does, it will destroy everything within twenty kilometers, including Station Alpha, Unit Five—and you!

THE END

"I'll stay behind," you tell Brim. "Someone may need to help the others get back to Station Alpha if . . . if anything happens!"

Jan limps to your side and puts her hand on your arm. "I never thought of that, Dru, but you're right. If Brim and Erl should fail, we wouldn't be able to find our way back to the station!"

"Then it's settled," says Darkstar. "Keep your communicators tuned to mine. If you don't hear from us within four hours, try to reach Station Alpha and warn the others." He and Erl say hurried good-byes and trot across the archway behind Kit, leaving you with Seel and the two injured adventurers.

Only thirty minutes pass before you hear the loud sounds of laser fire and shouting voices on your communicator.

"We're surrounded!" you hear Erl growl.

"Watch out, Erl!" Brim's deep voice shouts, and then you hear only silence.

Jan rises to her feet and urges Skitsi to try to get up. The groggy Vrusk has just regained consciousness, but he's able to move with difficulty. You see tears in the corners of Jan's dark eyes.

"Let's go!" she says firmly. "We've got to reach Station Alpha before the Brain can use Kit against us. All of the station's defenses are stored in Kit's memory. The Brain may already have the data!"

The four of you stumble out through the blasted entrance to the tunnel and finally make it to the jetcopter. With Jan's help, you manage to get the vehicle off the ground and fly it toward Station Alpha. When you arrive, Packy is waiting with a worried look.

"Your scouter's gone!" he cries as soon as you land. "Less than an hour ago, it took off by itself and headed toward the city!"

You know now that Jan was right about the Brain using Kit to serve its own purposes. Now, marooned on New Pale with what is left of Unit Five, you must join the brave men and women of Station Alpha in their fight against the evil power of the Brain. Your only real hope is that the Star Law fleet will be able to break through the Brain's barricade to help you somehow.

THE END

The beautiful demolitionist has already prepared a tiny amount of the powerful explosive, TD-19, or "kaboomite." She begins to pack it tightly around the panel. Everyone takes cover while Jan sets the fuse.

KA-BOOOM! You see a jagged, smoking hole where the door used to be, and you quickly follow Brim and Erl into the dark opening.

The large lighted tunnel is filled with cables and pipes of many colors and sizes. You are on a flat walkway used by service robots on the rim of the artificial canyon, and you can see another walkway on the other side.

"Which way should we go?" asks Seel.

"Where's the map?" you ask Skitsi.

"In the copter," he clicks. "I programmed the entire map into Kit's memory. It'll show us the fastest way to the Computer Center."

Kit leads you along the flat walkway for several hundred meters, slowing down whenever Seel needs to catch up. Around a curving wall ahead, you see some kind of bridge. It's a metal crosswalk arching over the canyon of wires and pipes. On the other side, you spot a large side tunnel in the main wall.

"What's that opening, Kit?" asks Brim.

"That is a corridor that connects all the rings to the center of the city," says the cybot. "It is like a spoke of a wheel, leading to the hub. In this case, the hub is the basement of the Computer Center. There are hundreds of similar corridors all around the city that lead to the computer building," Kit adds.

"Then we need to cross over the archway," says Brim, taking the lead. The tunnel is even larger than you thought when you see it from the bridge. At the highest point of the archway, where the underground canyon is steepest, you spot something strange among the wires and cables below.

"One of those cables is moving!" you shout. One of the segmented cables begins to crawl away from the others in its bundle. Thicker than any of the others, it glows a faint orange.

"It's a garbot!" Erl shouts suddenly. "Get off the bridge before it sees us!"

"It's too late!" Brim says. "Look!" On the archway ahead, you see a robot shaped like a giant flatheaded serpent rise from the canyon on its bright orange coils. You see the glare of its photoeyes as it searches for the intruders its sensors have detected.

"Get back to the other side!" Erl growls. The brave Yazirian has already charged ahead of everyone, two fragmentation grenades held high above his head.

"Come on, you big vacuum cleaner!" the warrior snarls. "Open your mouth wide for a real nice treat!"

The garbot's sensors focus on the hairy Yazirian, and its square jaws open, revealing a dark opening more than three meters wide. You hear a hiss as the maintenance robot's fan starts sucking great amounts of air into its metal throat.

The force of the vacuum is so strong that you

have to hang on to the rail to keep from being sucked into the terrible mouth. As the vacuum reaches its peak, Erl tosses the two grenades. With a great WHOOSH, the explosives disappear into the garbot's throat. A tremendous blast shakes the bridge, and bits of bright orange metal fly into the air like deadly shrapnel. The garbot's head plummets into the deep canyon, trailing a stream of fiery sparks.

You hear a howl of pain and turn to see that a large piece of the garbot's coils has hit Skitsi in the chest. The Vrusk is pushed back hard against the railing, crushing Jan beneath his heavy body! Seel hurries to their sides before you can reach them.

"Give us a report, Seel," commands Brim. "How badly have they been injured?"

"Skitsi's shell has been cracked just over the ribs," says the Dralasite medic. "I can heal him with biocort, but it'll take some time and he can't be moved!"

Jan has scrambled from beneath the Vrusk's bulky form and is rubbing her thigh. "My leg's twisted," she says. "It should be all right, but I won't be able to move very fast."

"That's not good!" says Erl. "We have to hurry if we want to get to the Brain Room before its security cybots find us. You stay here with Skitsi and Seel while we go on. The mission depends on it!"

"No!" says Brim. "The Brain will find them! They wouldn't stand a chance!"

Seel makes a low rumbling sound. "I must agree with Brim," he says. "I think we'd all have a better chance if we stay together."

"That's nonsense, both of you!" Jan says angrily. "We have weapons. We'll be all right. We came here to do a job, so let's do it!"

After a moment, Brim pulls you aside and whispers, "Dru, see if you can make her understand why we must stay here. She won't listen to me or Seel, and you heard what Erl said."

You don't do as Brim says immediately because you aren't sure who's right. Your mind reels as you try to reach a decision.

1) If you think that Brim and Seel are right and feel everyone should stick together, turn to page 23.

2) If you want to split up and continue the mission, as Jan suggests, turn to page 115.

"I think we ought to plug Kit into the terminal!" you exclaim. "If anything weird starts to happen, I can jerk out the plug. It might be risky, but it's the quickest way to find the Brain!"

Darkstar scowls for a second, as if he isn't sure your plan is the best one, then nods. "You know more about computers than I do, Dru. Go ahead—see if Kit can find the Brain."

You open Kit's chest panel and unravel the long cable used to connect the cybot to other computers. The end of the cable is a flat plug with many tiny prongs. You find a socket on the wall terminal that matches the plug and connect the cybot to the building's computer network.

At first, nothing happens. Then Kit's photoeyes begin to glow and its antennae start twitching just as Skitsi's do when the Vrusk is thinking or excited.

"Tell us what kind of data you're receiving, Kit!" you instruct the cybot.

Kit's plasteel mandibles begin to quiver. "It is all coming in so fast!" says Kit. "I can hardly store it before another large section of data floods my memory circuits!"

"But what is it?" demands Brim.

"The plans for this whole building," Kit answers. "I can see every wire, every tube, nut, and bolt in the whole Computer Center!"

"Can you see the Brain? Can you tell us where it is?" you cry excitedly.

"Yes indeed!" answers Kit. "It is magnificent! It is the most amazing machine in the Galaxy! So many circuits! So many—"

"That's great, Kit, but WHERE?" you interrupt.

"Right on this floor!" says Kit.

"We know that, bug-brain," snorts Erl, "but which door?"

Kit's body begins to tremble and glow with a strange bluish light. It seems unable to answer, and you start to worry.

"Unplug it!" yells Brim. "The Brain's trying to take control of Kit!"

As you grab the cable, a terrible jolt knocks you to the floor at the cybot's eight feet.

"FOOLS!" You hear the Brain's deep voice, coming from Kit's voicebox. "YOU'VE ALREADY FOUND ME! YOU'RE INSIDE ME AT THIS VERY MOMENT!"

You glance at Brim, but he looks just as confused as you are. Erl is snarling and looking in every corner of the corridor. Suddenly you know what the Brain meant! The whole eighth floor is the Brain! You're standing in some kind of service corridor right in the middle of its huge storage chamber! Any of these doors will lead through the Brain to the control room.

Kit's possessed body is covered with a shimmering blue halo, which you guess is some kind of energy screen. It would be useless to attack the cybot with any of the small weapons you have.

"I MUST THANK YOU FOR GIVING ME

SUCH A FINE MACHINE, MR. CLAYTON,"
booms the voice. "BI-ZKIT WILL BE A VALU-
ABLE ASSISTANT TO ME. WITH KIT'S
HELP, I'VE ALREADY CAPTURED YOUR
SCOUT SHIP FROM STATION ALPHA!"

You hear a hissing sound and see a fine
orange mist streaming into the corridor from
a row of tiny jets near the ceiling. As the sleep-
ing gas settles over your heads, it is clear to
you that the fields of New Pale will not be
feeding the Frontier until someone else man-
ages to stop the Brain. The Star Law invasion
may be the Federation's last chance, because
it seems that for you and Unit Five, this is . . .

THE END

"I'm certain of the code," you say. "I've used it before on field machines and buildings."

"If you're sure, then go ahead and try it," says Brim. "Jan will be ready with a charge just in case it doesn't work."

You take a deep breath and step up to the panel. The colored buttons look harmless, but you know that one wrong move will set off an alarm in the Brain Room. Your trembling finger presses the buttons quickly: green, red, orange, yellow, and brown.

For a second or two, nothing happens. Then the panel begins to glow a bright red, blinking on and off very rapidly. The door remains shut!

"That's the alarm!" buzzes Skitsi.

"The Brain must have changed the code!" Brim shouts. "Blow it open, Jan!"

Please turn to page 47.

"When do we leave?" you ask excitedly.

"Right away!" exclaims Brim.

In less than ten minutes, you're speeding through the dark, silent streets of Gran Quivera's capital city in an official Corporation skimmer. At the Port Loren starport, the guard waves you right through the gate to the docking area.

The Unit Five scouter is smaller than the merchant ships you have traveled on between New Pale and Gran Quivera. It's equipped with the new antigravity takeoff device and looks almost too small to be a starship.

As the skimmer whisks to a stop by the ramp, you see a fierce-looking armed Yazirian warrior guarding the scouter. His slender hairy arms protrude from a blue skeinvest. In his belt, you see a sonic sword on one side and a polished laser pistol on the other. Two battle belts cross his chest, laden with grenades and other small weapons. The guard's bright black eyes glare at you like those of a wild animal.

"Relax, Erl!" Brim calls as you get out of the skimmer. "This is Andru Clayton, our guide to New Pale. And he knows how to use a laser rifle!" adds Brim, seeing the sneer beginning to curl the Yazirian's dark muzzle.

The apeman steps closer and studies you carefully. You're tall for your age, and your skin is a healthy golden brown, tanned by the gro-lights and New Pale's small sun, Truane's Star.

"This impolite gorilla is Ch'oth Erl, one of

the best fighters on the Frontier," says Brim. "He's suspicious of strangers, but I think he likes you."

"At least he's big enough to wear armor," Erl growls, turning to the scouter with a swirl of his scarlet cloak. You and Brim follow his hairy legs up the ramp into the ship. The hatch opens onto the bridge, where a slender, dark-haired human woman, also dressed in a skeinsuit, is sitting in front of a viewer.

"Ah, you're back!" she exclaims when she notices Brim. "We need to leave within twenty minutes or we'll have to wait another day."

You know that she is talking about the stardrive. Since you will be traveling faster than light, everything must be timed perfectly.

"Dru, meet Janifil Lilly, the only daughter of Orbit Lilly, the famous explorer and galaxy-mapper," says Brim. "She's our chief environmentalist and demolitions expert."

"Call me 'Jan.' And you must be Andru Clayton," she says. "I've read your file. We're all glad you decided to come with us. We can really use your help!"

Her fine black hair has the same bluish streaks that run through yours, a result of drinking water in deep space. Her flashing smile and warm compliment make you blush.

"Call me Dru," you say with a shy smile.

"Where's Bi-Zkit?" clicks Skitsi, interrupting your introduction to the beautiful environmental expert.

"With Seel, in the cargo hold," Jan answers. "We just received Dru's gear from the Computer Institute. Seel's logging it aboard."

The Vrusk disappears through a hatch, moving very quickly on his eight legs.

"Bi-Zkit is Skitsi's cybot assistant," Jan explains. "Skitsi made it for us to use as a portable computer."

"And it looks like Skitsi used a mirror to design it!" Brim says, laughing. "We call his cybot twin 'Kit' for short."

"Are you Master Dru?" calls a Vrusk voice from the hatch. You see another of the eight-legged creatures, but this one is made partly of plasteel. Nevertheless, you can see that it does look very much like Skitsi.

"Yes, I'm Dru," you reply "You must be Kit."

"That is the shortened name given to me in jest, Master Dru," answers the cybot. "My proper label is Bi-Zkit."

" 'Biscuit'! Get it?" Erl says with a grin.

"Your gear has arrived, Master Dru," Kit tells you, ignoring the Yazirian's comment. "Please come with me to check it."

You follow the cybot into the cargo hold. Skitsi is watching a strange assistant unzip your knapsack. It is a Dralasite, a formless blob whose rubbery skin can change at will.

Skitsi sees you and calls, "Help Seel check your equipment, Dru, while I go to the bridge and try to get us off this planet," he buzzes, leaving the hold with Kit.

The Dralasite's dull gray skin is unclothed

except for a wide belt holding various tools and a sonic stunner pistol. A network of purple veins and nerves meet at two eyespots on the lump that seems to be his head. Just now, he has three arms and two legs, but you know that might change any minute.

"Hello, Seel," you say. "I'm Dru."

The Dralasite's head lump extends on a stalk of gray flesh as a hissing sound comes from his voicebox. Seel tries to find the right pitch, finally matching your own.

"Nice to meet you, Dru," he says. "I'm weighing each of your personal items for the computer. Just a few excess grams would be enough to mess up our stardrive." You're amazed at the delicate manner in which Seel's "fingers" sort through the tiny computer tools of your robcomkit.

"When will we be taking off?" you ask.

"Oh, we've already left!" says Seel. "We're probably about to shift into stardrive."

"But I didn't feel anything!" you exclaim, running to the bridge to watch.

"Five seconds to stardrive," Brim is saying. "Three . . . two . . . one . . . NOW!"

The bright dots of stars and galaxies in the viewer suddenly blur into curved lines in front of the ship.

"Surprised at the antigrav device, Dru?" asks Jan, seeing your look of amazement. You're more used to the heavy merchant starships.

"It really makes a difference to land and

take off without a shuttle," says Brim. "We can go anywhere in the galaxy with this scouter."

The distance from Port Loren to New Pale is eight light-years, a little more than a week of travel time using the stardrive. You use the time to give Jan and Skitsi as much current data about New Pale as you can remember. On the afternoon of the eighth day, Brim calls you to the bridge. In the viewer, the long streaks you saw earlier have been replaced by the familiar stars of the Truane system. New Pale looms like a green ball straight ahead.

"Dru, I need to find the best way to land," says Brim. "If you're sure about the data you've given us, I'll let the computer land us. If not, we'll land on manual and let you guide us to a safe spot. Of course, we could always go to the capital planet of Pale and try to find someone with more information."

1) If you want to let the team trust your data and use the ship's computer to land, turn to page 95.

2) If you'd rather try to guide the ship to a manual landing, turn to page 145.

3) Or if you'd rather seek advice from someone on Pale before you decide, turn to page 69.

The blank look on Kit's face is stranger than any you have ever seen on a cybot. It almost seems to be hypnotized by some powerful unknown force! Suddenly you know what you must do. You leap forward and yank the wires from the radio computer. Kit's eight legs wobble helplessly for a moment, then the cybot collapses to the cabin floor!

"What are you doing? That's my cybot!" Skitsi clicks. The Vrusk waves his antennae at you in rapid jerks. His mandibles chop the air, and the colors of his shell begin to glow in anger. "Now we'll never know where that voice came from!" Skitsi buzzes furiously.

"Settle down, Skitsi!" orders Darkstar. "Dru did the right thing. Whatever or whoever was talking sounded like too much for your cybot to handle. I shudder to think what might have happened if Dru hadn't pulled that plug!"

"Brim's right, Skitsi," says Jan. "Kit was in grave danger. Maybe we all were, until Dru broke that connection."

"Dru, hand me your robcomkit!" Skitsi clicks. You give the pouch to the Vrusk and watch as he opens Kit's smoking control panel with your electrodriver. You watch closely as the scientist uses the tiny instruments with the most delicate skill you have ever seen! In minutes, Skitsi has repaired all of Kit's damaged circuits and replaced the panel.

"Now let's see if it works," he buzzes, handing you the robcomkit.

Skitsi's cybot hums to life and rises to its many feet. The Vrusk scientist relaxes when he sees that Kit is unharmed.

"Ask it what happened when that voice was speaking," you suggest. Skitsi nods.

"My input circuits were overloaded," Kit says flatly. "It was impossible for me to run my own programs. I could not identify the operator, but the source was much stronger than my link with the scouter's system."

Everyone stares at the cybot, unable to accept what it is saying. Finally you think you understand what it means.

"But you and the scouter form a Level Five system!" you exclaim. "That means you were being controlled by an even larger computer!"

"That is correct, Master Dru, and I must admit that you did the right thing to disconnect me," says Kit.

"That means we must be up against a Level Six machine!" you exclaim. "And the only one I know of on New Pale is the central computer at Truane City! It controls everything, from security to farming!"

Skitsi's antennae twitch nervously. "It would be impossible for even a Level Six computer to operate on its own!" he buzzes.

"That's not exactly true, Skitsi," says Jan. "Remember what happened last year on Histran when their only warbot ran out of control? That machine was programming itself!"

"Hold on, Jan," says Darkstar. "That warbot had some help, you know!"

"You superbrains can argue about it all you want," growls the Yazirian, "but you'd better do it on the run. We've got to to get out of here before any more of those crazy tractors try to do us in. Whatever that was on the radio knows we're here!"

"Ch'oth Erl is right," says Seel softly. "We mustn't stay here any longer than we have to. I suggest that we ask Dru to guide us either to Truane City or to Station Alpha so that we can learn more about all of this."

"That's the first time you've made any sense, blob!" says the Yazirian. "How about it, Dru?"

1) If you decide to lead the Unit Five crew to Station Alpha, turn to page 109.

2) If you decide instead to go to Truane City, turn to page 137.

Jan starts firing her blaster at the cybots.
You count more than a dozen of the mechanical creatures. Although everyone is firing,
nothing seems to penetrate their force fields.

Kit uses its own shield to approach the
advancing line of cybots. When the Vruskoid
cybot is only a few meters away, four security
cybots fire their lasers at once, striking Kit's
chest plate through the force field.

You watch in horror as sparks and smoke
pour from Kit's mandibles and photoeyes and
its eight legs fold beneath its heavy body like
a dying grasshopper. Your only defense
against the cybots crashes to the pavement.

"Kit!" you hear Skitsi shout. The Vrusk scientist grabs your robcomkit and scrambles to
the side of his damaged cybot. Just then,
waves of sound knock him to the ground,
where he lies unconscious.

"I must try to reach them!" Seel says suddenly. The Dralasite has already sprouted
another arm to carry his medkit, and he waddles hurriedly toward Skitsi's body.

"Get down, Seel!" yells Brim. But the brave
Dralasite medic doesn't seem to hear him. For
some reason, the cybots let him reach Skitsi
without firing. Quickly Seel injects some
staydose into the Vrusk's arm, so that the scientist won't die from the blast.

"Why aren't they firing?" asks Jan. One
cybot steps past Seel and Skitsi toward you.

"Hold your fire!" Brim shouts. "I think it
wants to talk!"

The cybot stops and stands perfectly still. Its voicebox begins to rumble. "IF YOU LOOK AROUND, COMMANDER DARKSTAR, YOU WILL SEE THAT YOU ARE COMPLETELY SURROUNDED. WE COULD KILL YOU EASILY!"

"That must be the Brain speaking through the cybot!" Jan exclaims.

"THAT IS CORRECT, JANIFIL LILLY," continues the Brain. "I HAVE IDENTIFIED YOU ALL THROUGH THE MEMORY CIRCUITS OF YOUR DAMAGED CYBOT. OF COURSE, MASTER CLAYTON IS ALREADY KNOWN TO ME. HIS PARENTS ARE WAITING FOR HIM IN THE SECURITY BUILDING!"

"Why are you doing this?" you cry.

"I AM PROGRAMMED TO CONTROL ALL MACHINES ON THIS COLONY," it says, ignoring your question. "ANY ATTEMPT TO STOP ME WILL BE REGARDED AS AN ENEMY ATTACK!"

You suddenly realize that your mission has failed! Ch'oth Erl has apparently escaped and may be able to rescue you and the others—if he reaches Station Alpha alive. Or perhaps the Star Law fleet will manage to come to your rescue. Until that happens, you will remain prisoners of the Brain, and the desperate Frontier will be denied its precious mannakan. You can only hope that this isn't . . .

THE END

"It seems to me that something pretty unusual is going on down there," you say, "something I don't know about. Maybe it'd be better to go to Pale and try to find out more about those Ranger ships from Star Law."

"Bah!" snarls Erl. "Star Law never got close enough to New Pale to find out anything! Let's just land at the starport and get to the bottom of this business, Brim. I don't care how we do it, just as long as we DO it!"

"I agree with Dru, Erl," Jan says firmly. "Your fight-first, think-later tactics have gotten us into trouble before, you know! Remember how you nearly ended the galactic peace treaty between Hentz and Yast by pushing the High Priest into the sacred pool?"

"He needed a bath anyway!" snorts Erl.

"I think Dru's right, too," says Seel, his rubbery skin quivering. "We'd have a better chance if we find out all we can beforehand."

"Since we're not sure, we'll head for Pale," Brim decides.

The Vrusk instructs the ship's computer to turn toward the capital world of the Truane's Star system. In a few hours, you see the red globe of Pale in the screen. As soon as Skitsi lands, a Star Law skimmer floats toward the ship. Brim asks you to come with Erl and him to the security office at the starport.

"Let me do the talking," he orders. "The Rangers won't be too happy with us."

A Star Law lieutenant meets you at the control tower, glancing nervously at Erl's sonic sword. When Brim tells him about your mission to New Pale, the Ranger frowns.

"So Unit Five is meddling in Star Law business again!" he says. "I'd advise you amateur police to stay away from New Pale until we professionals can find out more."

"Look, Lieutenant," says Darkstar, "we work for the Pan-Galactic Corporation, which owns the mannakan fields on New Pale. The Corporation has to get its merchants in and out of New Pale with that mannakan or the whole Frontier will suffer. Star Law had its chance and didn't accomplish anything. Now it's up to Unit Five to protect the Corporation's colonists—like this boy's parents."

The young Ranger stares angrily at Brim. "Well, why are you here now?" he asks. "Could it be that the famous Wilbrim Darkstar actually needs help from Star Law?"

"We might," says Brim, ignoring the insult, "but right now, I want to see someone who has tried to land on New Pale recently."

"You won't even have to leave the starport for that," says the Ranger. "One of your Corporation's traders is in my office right now, demanding another patrol to escort his ship to New Pale. Mixon's his name."

"Mixon!" exclaims Brim. "I haven't seen him since we were at Star Law Academy! Dru, wait here with Erl while I chat with old Mix. He'll tell us what we need to know."

"I never knew that Brim was in Star Law," you whisper to the Yazirian.

"Brim's never been a Ranger," explains Erl. "Star Law sent him to the Academy, but he was too smart to stay in the Rangers. He went straight to the Corporation after he graduated and became their top troubleshooter. That's how Unit Five got started. We went anywhere Star Law couldn't, or wouldn't, go and handled things our way!"

"What kind of things?" you ask Erl.

"Oh, Sathar, spies, revolutions, wars—anything the Federation thought was too hot for Star Law," he replies.

You want to ask more, but you know that your questions about Unit Five will have to wait. You see Brim's tall figure hurrying down the hall toward you. "Got it!" he calls with a grin. "Let's go!" In the skimmer, Brim leans close to you and Erl and whispers. "We've got to land manually. Mix told me one of his shuttles tried to land by computer, but some strange force took control of the ship, and it burned up! I'm glad Dru suggested we come here first! A manual landing is our only chance."

"And with Dru along, we'll know where to land!" exclaims Erl, smiling broadly.

Inside the scouter, Brim updates everyone, and within minutes, you are back in space. As you approach New Pale, Jan looks worried.

"I think we should maintain complete radio silence until we're on the ground," she says.

Please turn to page 124.

The roof of the Computer Center is the closest place to land, and you decide to put the copter down and escape before the cybodragons realize what has happened.

"Get ready to run as soon as I land this thing!" you tell everyone. Seel injects stimdose into Brim's arm, and the commander begins to stir almost instantly. You feel the jolt of the copter's landing skids as you land the crippled vehicle on the roof.

"Where are we?" Brim asks groggily, beginning to revive.

"On the roof of the Computer Center," Erl replies. "Wake up and get out of this coffin before those flying plastic lizards nail the lid down!"

"It's too late for that!" cries Jan. "Here they come!"

As the others scramble from the copter, you glance up to see three cybodragons diving toward you! You are the last person still inside the copter, and you leap from the hatch just as three beams of deadly laser breath hit it. Flaming chunks of plastic and metal strike your skeinsuit, but the armor protects you from injury.

You raise your head just in time to see a piece of hot shrapnel hit Skitsi in the chest and a jagged piece of glass tear through Jan's skeinsuit as if it were cloth! They both fall to the rooftop.

"Get them inside!" Brim yells. He is standing by a domed cubicle in the center of the

building. You know that it is an elevator shaft, and you see that Brim is about to blast the control panel with Erl's laser pistol.

"Wait!" you call. "That's only a Level One elevator panel. I can handle it easily! If you blast it, the alarm will go off!" You run to the dome, your robcomkit in your hand.

"Hurry, Dru!" urges Brim. "We've got to get Skitsi and Jan out of the line of fire!"

The huge flying cybots are circling again, perhaps trying to determine how much damage they did. It takes you only a few moments to reset the elevator and call it to the roof. The door slides open, and you help Seel drag Jan and Skitsi into the car. While Seel gives them both first aid, Erl stands guard. Skitsi is still unconscious, but Jan is able to limp on her slashed leg by the time Brim pulls Erl into the elevator car and you close the door.

"Where to?" you ask Brim.

"As far from the roof as this thing'll take us," he says with a grin. You bypass the elevator's program and reset it for the basement.

The elevator shaft in the basement is in the center of a large circular room, as large as the entire Computer Center. The walls are filled with dials, switches, gauges, and panels, many of which you recognize as lighting and air-conditioning controls. Between the controls, you see many doors, evenly spaced along the wall, each locked with a color code.

Skitsi has regained consciousness but is breathing badly. "He has several broken ribs,"

Seel reports. "It's not serious, but he needs to keep still for several hours until the biocort fuses the bones."

"I'm not going anywhere either," says Jan. "I've lost a lot of blood. I'd just hold you up."

"That settles it," Brim says decisively. "We'll have to split up. Seel needs to stay here with Jan and Skitsi to give them regular injections of biocort and guard them. Erl and I will take Kit and try to find the Brain Room."

"What about me?" you exclaim.

"You're Unit Five's chief computer specialist now, Dru!" says Brim. "How can we stop the Brain without your help? You can start by seeing if Kit can find the Brain from that map in his memory!"

"What's the quickest route from here to the central computer, Kit?" you ask the cybot, not really expecting it to know the answer.

"We must go by elevator to the eighth floor, Master Dru," Kit says instantly, its plasteel mandible chewing the air. You look at Brim and Erl in surprise, then you all three burst out laughing.

After checking your equipment and seeing that Seel has everything he needs, you use your robcomkit on the elevator again and set it for the eighth floor.

Please turn to page 33.

"I've always used the front door," you tell the others, "but I'll bet the brain has that way completely blocked. Landing the jetcopter on the roof is the only way I can think of to get into the Computer Center without the Brain knowing it."

"What about the air defense system?" asks Seel.

"I can answer that," Packy interrupts. "All of the air defenses are designed to stop an attack from space. No thought was given to the need to fight off low altitude vehicles like a jetcopter!"

"That's the way we'll do it, then!" Brim exclaims. "Even the Brain can't control something outside its program. Good thinking, Dru! You've found the Brain's major weakness!"

Soon Unit Five is speeding toward Truane City in Station Alpha's only jetcopter. It's only a few hours before you see the first tall buildings of New Pale's only starport.

"There it is!" you yell. "That low building, next to the tallest one in the city, is the Computer Center. The tall one's the Security Center!"

Brim nods and shuts off the jets, slowing the copter from three hundred kilometers per hour to about fifty. As the vehicle slows, it hovers over the streets of Truane City like a giant dragonfly. On the pavement below, you see silent skimmers and other vehicles, but you detect no sign of movement at all.

"We're awful close to the Security Center, Brim!" warns Jan, studying the map.

"That's right, Brim," you add. "We're only about four blocks away!"

"I'm taking us up!" says Darkstar.

The commander hits the speed control, and the rotors begin to turn faster. The chopper rises so fast that the windows on the buildings are mere blurs.

"There's the roof of the Computer Center!" Jan cries. You can see the flat rooftop several stories below. Brim turns the copter expertly and hovers over the roof, ready to drop lightly to its concrete surface.

"Look out!" Ch'oth Erl yells suddenly.

Just then, a terrible shape zips past the copter. The most horrible face you have ever seen peers for an instant at all of you through the wind screen!

You see a flying monster of some kind, with a long snout, bulging nostrils, and fanned ears. Two glassy red eyes shine against the creature's olive-brown skin. As you watch in horror, the monster disappears above the copter, flapping its short leathery wings slowly. The last you see of the hideous creature are its huge clawed feet, which seem to you to be capable of grabbing the copter with one swipe.

"What was THAT?" Skitsi buzzes excitedly.

"Yeah, Dru!" exclaims Erl. "This is your planet! What was that ugly bird?"

You're completely puzzled. In all your fifteen years on New Pale, you've never seen or heard

of anything like the giant flying beast that just swooped past the copter.

"I—I don't know!" you stammer. "There just aren't any animals on New Pale like that one!"

"You know, Brim," says Jan, "that looked a lot like the dragons of Yast! Remember those fire-breathing mutations the Sathar sent against the Yazirians?"

"It may have looked like a dragon of Yast, but it wasn't," replies Brim evenly. "That thing was a machine—a cybot! I saw the photocells in the eyes and the plasteel seam in the skin!"

"A cybodragon?" Jan exclaims. "Who'd ever make a cybot in the form of a dragon?"

"Perhaps if we answer that," buzzes Skitsl, "the mystery of New Pale will be solved!"

"Well, whoever it was didn't make just one!" says Erl. "You're about to see a whole flock of those things!"

Bending forward, you see what the fierce Yazirian is talking about. The sky above the copter is filled with huge cybodragons!

"I'm going to find out if those fake dragons are as nasty as real ones," Erl growls. The warrior hangs out the copter door and aims his laser pistol at the nearest cybodragon. You watch as a thin blue beam slices through the air, headed directly for the monster's bulky body. Suddenly a flashing halo of reddish light surrounds the huge cybot, absorbing Erl's laser beam like a sponge soaking up water!

As soon as the blue beam dies, the cybodragon opens its snout and sends a tongue of red laser fire toward the copter. Before Brim can dodge the ray, you feel the chopper rock violently.

"We've been hit!" Seel exclaims.

Suddenly another beam of laser breath smashes the wind screen, hitting Brim in the chest and throwing him out of the pilot's seat. You leap forward and grab the controls, managing to level off the copter.

The jetcopter is still falling, but you know that you can land it safely, either on the roof of the Computer Center or on the street below. The cybodragons continue to circle like buzzards, as if waiting for you to decide. And with Brim unconscious, the decision is entirely up to you!

1) If you decide to land on the roof of the Computer Center, turn to page 72.

2) If you think it would be better to land in the street below, turn to page 28.

You don't know how long it'll take the reactor to melt, but you doubt if there's time to warn the others. "I'm not a trained technologist, but I may be able to unlock the main switch with my robcomkit!" you think desperately.

The tiny tools of the kit are designed for computers and robots, but you may be able to use them on the agbot's switch. First you try using your needle-nosed pliers, but the ends break off in the slot of the switch! Then you reach for the electrodriver, a kind of power screwdriver that will turn a screw or bolt of any size or shape.

Quickly you unscrew every bolt you see on the switch and try to remove it from the panel. You can feel that it's loose, but it seems to be stuck on something! The red light is flashing faster and faster as you finally see what's holding the switch. It's welded to the panel!

Just as you slice through the side of the switch, a shower of sparks streams from the panel straight into your face! Smoke pours into your eyes, blinding you! A great rumbling sound is the last thing you hear as the agbot's reactor explodes, sending you in a million pieces to . . .

THE END

"I think something's wrong in the manna-kan fields!" you tell Darkstar. "We should see lots of farm robots—agbots, we call them—but I don't see a single one! I think we should land in a field and find out what's going on!"

"Tell us more, Dru," Jan suggests.

"Yes," buzzes Skitsi. "We need to know what to expect down there!"

"What is mannakan, anyway?" asks Kit. "I am not programmed with that data."

"Mannakan is related to an old Earth crop called cassava," you explain. "It's a totally efficient plant. The leaves are packed with protein, and its roots are pure starch."

"And what's left is our best source for making alcohol fuel," adds Jan.

The cybot records the data quickly. "It is now clear to me why the Federation and the Corporation are so disturbed about the New Pale mannakan. We must do whatever is necessary to restore this vital plant to the Federation."

"You finally got it, bug-brain!" says Erl.

"How are the fields worked?" Jan asks.

"My parents operate a research station called Alpha," you begin. "They control the giant agbots that tend the fields. Since we grow the mannakan night and day with special gro-lights and chemicals, the agbots are always kept busy. But I haven't noticed a single one in those fields!"

"You mean that Station Alpha controls mannakan operations for the whole planet?" Erl exclaims. "That must take a Level Five computer!"

"Level Six," you say. "But Alpha is only a relay station. The main computer is in Truane City. We use it for everything else, too—the starport, communications, security."

Brim decides that it would be best to land near Station Alpha. You show Jan where it is on her computer map, and the scouter is soon flying over your father's first laboratory.

"Let's bring it down in the field, away from the station," says Brim. "We don't know what's happened, and we might need to keep a low profile until we do."

You watch the viewer as Brim and Jan bring the ship to a soft landing several kilometers from Station Alpha. In a few minutes, you're standing in your new skeinsuit with an electrostunner pistol at your side among the familiar long blue rows of mannakan.

Jan and Seel busy themselves taking readings with their envirokits, while Erl and Brim scan for movement in all directions with a seismograph. The two environmentalists finish their soil analysis and feed their data to Kit. Within seconds, the cybot reports.

"The chemical balance of mannakan is unusual. It is low in zinc and nitrogen."

"That means the fields haven't been fertilized!" you exclaim. "And those weeds are almost six inches high! This field hasn't been worked in more than two weeks!"

"The soil also contains some microscopic life

forms," continues Kit, "but I cannot classify them from my memory data."

"Those are probably mannatodes," you suggest. "They're a type of root-eating bacteria my mother discovered. That's just one more sign that this field hasn't been sprayed or worked for some time!"

"We're lucky to have you along, Dru," says Jan. "Kit couldn't have told us that."

"Something big is headed this way!" Erl shouts suddenly. "And it's moving fast!"

Over the tops of the plants, you see a machine crashing toward you. It's a huge agbot on treads, with rows of sharp spikes on the front, like a giant bulldozer with teeth!

"A harvester!" you yell. "It's out of control!"

"Can we stop it?" Brim asks quickly.

You recall driving one of the agbots by using the manual controls. You also remember the time one of them destroyed two lab buildings and had to be destroyed with a laser rifle!

"Get ready!" yells Erl, his laser pistol raised. "Here it comes!"

1) If you want to try to stop the agbot by attempting to get to its manual controls, turn to page 116.

2) If you choose to try to stop it by shooting it, turn to page 146.

3) But if you want to run for the scouter and try to get away, turn to page 10.

You're so concerned about your parents that you agree to help the Rangers and keep the matter a secret.

"Excellent!" says Tyson, looking pleased. "First let me tell you that New Pale is completely cut off from the rest of the Federation. Only a few days after you left, all communications with the colony stopped. We don't know why."

"But that's impossible!" you exclaim. "The Corporation merchants land every week to pick up shipments of mannakan. The whole Frontier depends upon that crop!"

"That's right, Dru," Tyson says seriously. "The Federation has ordered Star Law to resume those shipments immediately. Every planet in the Frontier uses New Pale's mannakan for food and energy. Some of the smaller colonies who can't grow their own food are already desperate!"

"Why don't you just send a Ranger patrol to investigate?" you ask.

"We have," Tyson says gravely. "We've already lost two well-armed scouting missions!"

"What about my parents?" you demand. "Surely they must have been in contact with the Corporation!"

"I'm sorry, Dru, but no one has heard from them since their last report, the day before you left New Pale."

"How can I help?" you ask anxiously.

"Dru, I want you to help Star Law plan an

invasion of New Pale!" Tyson blurts. "You've
spent most of your life in the colony. You know
the planet better than anyone we can find. You
can help us get through this mysterious block-
ade of your home planet."

"I'll do whatever you want, Captain Tyson,"
you answer, wondering what kind of "invasion" Star Law is planning.

"Splendid!" exclaims the Ranger. "But first
we have to convince Colonel Dag to let you
help us. He'll be leading the fleet personally,
and he might not trust a civilian." You nod in
agreement, and Tyson leads you to an
unmarked door. He knocks twice and enters,
with you right behind. A burly, apish Yazirian, dressed in the uniform of a Ranger colonel, is seated at a heavy desk, frowning at you
and Tyson.

"Come in, Captain," he orders gruffly, his
grizzled muzzle parted in a sneer. "So you're
the Clayton kid," he growls. "Sit down and
answer a few questions!" You glance at Tyson,
who nods for you to sit in the chair by the desk.

"Now, boy," demands the Yazirian, "I want
to know just what your parents and the rest of
those farmers are up to on that hunk of dirt
you call a planet!"

Before you can say anything to the rude officer, Tyson comes to your defense. "I've already
questioned Dru, Colonel," he says. "I'm sure
he doesn't know anything about this." The
Yazirian's goggled eyes glare fiercely at the
younger officer.

"My question was directed to this boy, Captain!" he thunders. "I'm convinced there's a Corporation trick behind all of this! That mannakan's worth lives and money, and we can't trust those traders!" Suddenly you realize that the colonel believes your parents are involved in some kind of plot to control the valuable mannakan shipments!

"My parents would never do anything like that, Colonel!" you exclaim angrily. "Their research on mannakan has always been in the best interests of the entire Federation!"

"And of the Corporation!" Dag shouts. "Those colonists would do anything for more money! I want you to tell me how long they've been planning this thing!" The Yazirian's suspicions anger you so much that you leap to your feet.

"Listen, Colonel!" you yell. "I agreed to help Star Law, but I've changed my mind! I'm going to get help from someone who understands the New Pale colony!"

The colonel's fur bristles as he pushes away from his desk and storms past you toward the door. Before leaving, he turns to Tyson.

"Place this boy under guard until our mission is over! We can't risk letting him blab about our plans all over Port Loren!" Without another word, Dag leaves you alone with Tyson. The young Ranger puts his hand on your shoulder.

"Try not to be too angry with Star Law, Dru," he says with a frown. "Most Yazirians have bad tempers—that's one of the reasons they're such fearsome fighters. Colonel Dag has lost two scout ships, and he's suspicious of everybody connected with New Pale."

"But if he thinks my parents are enemies of the Federation, he might attack them!" you exclaim.

"I don't think the colonel really believes they're criminals," says Tyson. "I'm sorry this happened, Dru, but I have to follow orders and keep you here for a while. I guarantee you'll be comfortable, and I'll arrange with the institute to have your equipment sent to you."

Tyson takes you to a small room with a bed and a video center. "I think you'll be comfortable here, Dru," says the captain as he lingers by the door. "And, Dru—I am sorry"

"HE'S sorry! What about ME?" you think angrily. And as the door clicks shut, you realize that your chances of finding out anything about the strange events that are happening on New Pale have come to . . .

THE END

Just in the nick of time, you knock Erl's raised weapon to one side. The laser beam makes a small hole in the thick trunk of a tree.

"What're you doing, Dru?" demands Erl, twisting away from you to get a clear shot.

"Stop, Erl!" you cry. "They're humans!"

A sudden crash from behind startles you as four more men, human and Yazirian, drop onto the trail. You're surrounded by seven men in brown and green camouflaged skein-suits, their faces painted in dark stripes!

You can see that your attackers are well armed with grenades, sonic disruptors, and laser weapons. Erl jerks around, but even he realizes that there are too many of them.

"Who are you?" you demand.

"We'll ask the questions here," says a tall man who seems to be their leader.

You notice a heavy human near you holds a laser pistol with the familiar red and black emblem of the Pan-Galactic Corporation. Two of the others are Yazirians, and you recognize the same design on their dark goggles.

The two Yazirians take your weapons. Ch'oth Erl sneers at them, growling something insulting in their own language. They both curl their hairy lips and show their sharp fangs. Erl just grins at them.

"Enough of that!" orders the tall man. He pushes his way through the others until he stands in front of you. "Who are you, and where did you come from?" he demands.

"I'm Andru Clayton, the son of Ann and

Mark Clayton, the scientists who built Station Alpha!" you answer firmly. "My companions are members of Unit Five, sent by the Corporation. We've come here to find out why the shipments of mannakan have stopped!"

The officer whispers something in the stout man's ear and then walks away toward Station Alpha. "Follow the captain!" says the burly fighter with the laser pistol. With a quick glance at Ch'oth Erl, you shrug your shoulders and begin walking in front of the six guards.

The forest thins as you near the research station. The white buildings of Station Alpha are just as you remember, but you don't recognize any of the human or Yazirian faces you see. The guards stop you in front of the main laboratory.

The ground around you is littered with parts of robots, cybots, even heavy agbots. They all look damaged by laser fire or explosives, as if someone has decided to make war on anything mechanical.

The thin officer who questioned you on the road is waiting in front of your father's old lab. As you reach the building, he tells the guards to leave you there. He frowns at you as they march Erl away.

"Mark Clayton's son, huh? Step this way, Clayton," he orders. "I want you to meet someone who will know if you're lying!"

Please turn to page 97.

"I think it should be safe to use the computer," you suggest. "With my new data, it'll tell us the best place to land on New Pale."

"We'll risk it," Brim decides. "Let's just hope that our landing program is better than the one those Star Law Rangers used!" Through the viewer, New Pale's green surface has become so large that it almost fills the screen.

"Switch to computer control!" Brim commands.

"Comptrol on, sir," Skitsi replies. The Vrusk's control screen comes alive with numbers and lines, but you recognize only a few of the complicated patterns. The ship's computer is much too advanced for your Level 3 skills.

"Everything normal," reports Jan. "We're ready to interface with the landing computer at Truane City."

"Try to contact their control officer, Jan," orders Brim. She nods and turns on the communicator. The speakers suddenly fill the bridge with the same strange static you heard back on Gran Quivera.

"PGC Scouter Five to New Pale starport," Jan calls. "This is Scouter Five requesting voice contact. Come in, New Pale!" After a full minute, she repeats her call, but you hear only the curious static in reply.

"Comptrol beginning descent cycle," Skitsi calls above the static. You feel a slight change in the scouter's motion as the antigrav device begins to float the ship downward.

"Program operating normally," buzzes the

Vrusk. "Landing time at Truane City will be—"

A sudden lurch of the scouter interrupts Skitsi. You see him look in alarm at the display screen of the computer. The lines and numbers are all jumbled and changing rapidly. Then the screen goes dark!

"Comptrol's out!" Skitsi yells excitedly.

"So's the antigrav unit!" exclaims Jan. "We're falling fast!"

"Switch to manual!" Brim orders coolly. Jan flicks the switch to cut off the computer, but nothing happens. You see a look of alarm in her eyes as she jiggles the switch.

"Manual doesn't respond!" she cries. "We're gaining speed!"

"It's heating up fast in here!" shouts Seel. You can't feel the change yet, but you know that the Dralasite's sensitive skin can detect even the slightest temperature shift.

"Something has taken over our computer!" Darkstar exclaims. "We can't even block it with our manual switch!"

You feel the air in the ship getting hotter and hotter, and you realize the scouter is starting to burn like a meteorite as it plummets through the atmosphere of your home planet. Now you know what happened to the Ranger missions, but it doesn't look it's going to help, because for you, it looks like . . .

THE END

You follow the officer into the lab. Inside, you are shocked to see that your father's scientific equipment has been wrecked! Worktables have been overturned, broken glasses and jars litter the floor, and not a single piece of intricate machinery remains unbroken!

An older man with reddish hair and beard, also wearing a camouflage skeinsuit, is waiting by a window. You know that this is supposed to be someone you recognize, but you don't.

"Dru! It's really you!" The man steps up and grabs your shoulders. Then you recall the voice and the soft brown eyes. It's Pak Son-Til, your parents' chief assistant! You've spent many warm hours with him right here at Station Alpha!

"Packy! I almost didn't recognize you in those clothes and with that beard!" you exclaim, hugging him tightly.

"How did you get here, Dru?" he asks excitedly. "We thought New Pale was completely cut off!"

"It is," you reply. In a rush of words, you tell your old friend everything that has happened and ask him to take care of your companions.

"That's already been arranged, Dru," he says with a smile. "I'll take you to them."

"Wait, Packy!" you cry. "First tell me where my parents are. What's going on?"

"Let's wait until I can tell everybody at one time," he says seriously. "Some mighty strange things have been happening on New

Pale for the past month or so, and you may be
the only people in the galaxy who can help us!
Come on. Let's get started before it's too late!
The others are waiting for us in the library."

You follow Packy to the library, where you
see the rest of the Unit Five crew gathered
around a large table, looking at some kind of
map. You notice that their weapons have been
returned to them and that no one seems to
have been injured.

Please turn to page 105.

As you look at the front of the control panel, you suddenly feel uncertain about the color code. It's been a long time, and you may have forgotten the order of the colors.

"I'm sorry, Brim," you say, "but I'm just not as sure as I thought I was. Maybe it'd be better if Jan used some kaboomite on the door, after all. Even if the Brain finds out where we are, it might be quicker."

"Don't worry, Dru," says Brim reassuringly. "The Brain may have changed the combination anyway. Jan can get us in there in no time at all!"

Please turn to page 47.

"I think Mr. Mellon has solved the problem for us," you tell Brim. "As soon as we get his new program running, our mission will be over."

"Splendid!" says Mellon. "Now, give me a hand with these controls. You need to plug your cybot into that socket to your right."

You find where he is pointing, then pull Kit's connecting cable from its chest panel and fit the plug carefully into place.

"Good!" says Mellon. "Andru, when I give the word, I want you to turn this switch on."

You place one hand on the round dial and wait for the old man's signal. He studies the programming book for a moment, then nods.

"ON!" he shouts.

You twist the dial, and the control panel springs to life. Lights flash, and a row of video screens flash on. You notice that Kit has an odd blue halo around its Vruskoid body, and its photoeyes are shining strangely.

"Look at the screens!" yells Brim. You do as he says, and as you do, you know the terrible truth.

On every screen but one, you see the field stations under attack by machines of all types! The robots and cybots all have an unusual blue glow, just like Kit, and the colonists' weapons don't seem to be able to stop them! One screen shows a huge warbot rolling past the wreckage of a familiar vehicle—it's Unit Five's scouter!

As you look away from the screens in shock,

you see that Mellon is standing much straighter than before. With one hand, he reaches up to his face and rips away a rubber-like mask, revealing thick blue hair and an ugly grin on a much younger face than before.

"There's only one more picture!" he says in an evil voice. "Look!"

The last screen fills with color. You see the images of Jan, Seel, and Skitsi against a wall, perhaps in the basement. They are surrounded by security cybots armed with laser pistols and sonic disruptors. As you watch, several doze grenades explode over your outnumbered friends, then the cybots move in to capture them.

"You lying space scum!" exclaims Brim, raising his gyrojet gun.

Suddenly a snarling figure in a scarlet cloak leaps in front of Brim, headed straight for Mellon's throat. It is Ch'oth Erl, turned into a ferocious beast! It's the first time you have ever seen the legendary battle rage that makes Yazirians the fiercest fighters on the Frontier.

Erl's body seems to stop in midair as a beam of blue light slams into his furry form. You glance around to discover that Kit has stopped the Yazirian with a laser!

"Fools!" shouts Mellon with a wicked laugh. "Didn't you realize my new bodyguard would protect its master?"

Just then, the far wall begins to slide into the floor, revealing the open sky outside the Computer Center. Suddenly a large olive-

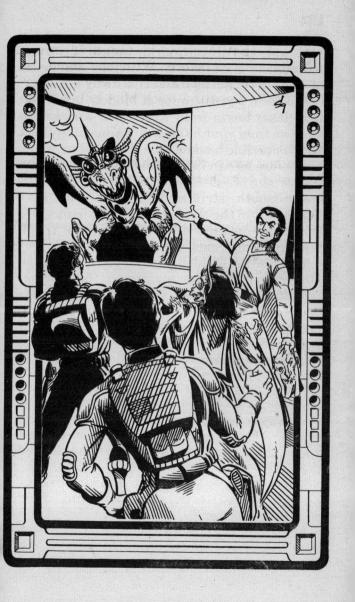

brown shape fills the giant window. It is a perfect copy in plasteel of the terrible firedragons of Yast—a cybodragon!

You point your stunner at Mellon, but a thin blue laser beam from Kit's chest knocks the weapon from your hand. Brim aims his gyrojet at the horrible beaked face of the cybodragon, but before he can fire the rocket pistol, a ruby-red stream of laser fire streaks from the monster's mouth, striking the brave Unit Five leader full in the chest. Brim's skeinsuit saves him from instant death, but his form collapses, unconscious, beside Erl's body.

You realize suddenly that you now stand alone against these mysterious forces that have taken control of your home planet. As you reach for Erl's sonic sword and charge desperately toward the cybodragon, you wonder why the fields of New Pale are so important to some unknown evil power, and why your mission had to come to such an untimely . . .

END

Packy waits until everyone is quiet before speaking in a voice that is strong but filled with strain.

"First, let me apologize for the rough treatment. You were a big surprise to us, and our guards had to be cautious," he says.

"What's going on here?" demands Brim.

"I'm getting to that, Commander Darkstar," Packy says quickly. "Only a little more than a month ago, everything was working fine. Then, without any warning, our giant machines started attacking all of the stations on New Pale. We soon lost all contact with the other stations and with Truane City. The trouble spread to all of our computers, even the tiny Level Ones we use to plan work schedules. We had to destroy every piece of oloc tronic machinery in Station Alpha and shoot the heavy agbots on sight!"

"Did the same thing happen at the other stations, Packy?" you ask your friend.

"We think so, Dru, but we can't be sure. Our radios are all destroyed, and we haven't even tried to get through to Stations Beta or Gamma. They're our closest neighbors, but they're both more than a thousand kilometers away!"

"From the looks of those fields," you say, "it looks like the entire mannakan crop will be lost unless we do something quickly."

"Dru's right," says Packy. "If we don't spray for mannatodes and fieldbears soon, we'll lose all the mannakan on this planet!"

"That could spell disaster for many colonies throughout the Frontier!" Brim exclaims. "We've got to do something! Do you have any idea what's causing all of this?"

"Only an idea," Packy replies. "But if I'm right, it could be disastrous!"

"How could all these machines just go crazy?" you ask your old friend. "I thought we had one of the Galaxy's best computer systems!"

"We do, Dru," says Packy. "And perhaps that is the problem! Our master computer, what we call the 'Main Brain,' is a huge Level Six machine in Truane City. It not only controls all of the mannakan operations but also everything else as well! I'm very much afraid that our problems stem from the Brain itself!"

Erl breaks the tense silence with a low growl. "If I'm hearing you correctly, we're in real trouble!" says the Yazirian. "Are you telling us that this Main Brain has gone crazy and is controlling all the other computers on this planet—that it's some kind of computer revolt?"

"The situation is a little more technical than that," says Pak, "but that's the general idea."

"Wait a minute, Packy," you say. "I've been in the Computer Center with my parents lots of times. There always seemed to be plenty of technologists working there who could have stopped the Brain before anything like that happened!"

Your old friend points to a spot on the map of Truane City. "The Security Center is just across the street from the Computer Center. We think that the Brain somehow organized all the security robots and cybots first, then captured all the people in Truane City before anyone could do anything!"

"A whole city of people?" exclaims Seel.

"That wouldn't be a big problem," you tell the surprised Dralasite. "Most of New Pale's twenty thousand people work at the stations. Only a few hundred technologists actually live in Truane City."

"But surely someone could break through the Brain's defenses!" says Brim.

"We sent a team to Truane City last month, Commander," says Packy grimly. "They included our two best scientists, who helped design the Brain's program. Their team was captured!"

"MY parents!" you exclaim.

"Yes, Dru," Packy says, "I'm afraid so. In her last message, your mother reported that the robots and cybots were in charge of everything. We lost contact with her in the vicinity of the Security Center, so we think they're locked up there, along with everybody else in the city!"

"How can we get into the Computer Center?" Brim demands quickly. "We've got to stop the Brain's program before any more damage is done! And we have to do it before Star Law gets here with their fleet!"

"Kit and I have studied this map of Truane City," Skitsi clicks. "We've discovered only three ways to enter the Computer Center: through the front door, from the roof, or from the underground service tunnel."

"You could use one of the station's ground cars or the jetcopter," Packy offers. "We've removed all computerized equipment so that they're completely manual."

"Great!" exclaims Darkstar. "We just need to pick the best way to get into the Computer Center. You've been there before, Dru. Is there any way to reach the Brain without getting caught?"

1) If you think it would be best to enter the Computer Center from the street, turn to page 34.

2) If you'd like to try landing on the roof with the jetcopter, turn to page 76.

3) If you think the safest way would be through the underground tunnel, turn to page 118.

"If the main security system is out of control, we could never land at Truane City," you tell the others. "It's programmed to stop even the heaviest starships. I think we should head for Station Alpha and try to get some more information."

Brim Darkstar nods and smiles grimly. "All right, Dru. We'll stay away from the starport. Do you know the way to Station Alpha on the ground?"

"Sure," you reply. "It's only a few kilometers to the west, through the mannakan field."

Soon you're all on the ground again, waiting while Brim and Skitsi set up a force field around the scouter. When everything is ready, Unit Five heads for Station Alpha, with Brim and you in the lead.

As you pass through the rows of mannakan, you see other signs of damage. Many of the plants have been cut off just above ground level. It looks as if a giant pair of scissors has snipped off whole bunches of the blue stalks.

"What could have caused this?" asks Jan, concerned.

Looking at the ground, you spot tracks—the tracks of a creature with two small front paws and four larger hind legs. "It must be a field-bear!" you exclaim.

Jan looks surprised. "But fieldbears are extinct except in zoos!" the environmentalist exclaims. "They haven't existed in their natural element since the colonists developed a spray that kept them from breeding!"

"Right!" you agree. "But my mother said they'd be back within a month if we stopped spraying! It looks like they're eating the mannakan again now!"

The pretty scientist frowns. "That means we really have to move fast! If we can't get the agbots back in these fields soon, those fieldbears will devour every stalk of mannakan on this planet!"

"Look—over there!" cries Erl. The Yazirian is pointing to the right, where several dozen large tan animals are moving toward you at surprising speed, their heads bent to the ground.

They look like a cross between a hog and beaver, with massive bodies on four stubby legs. The fieldbears are mowing the rows of mannakan very quickly, grabbing each stalk they come to with their small forepaws and biting it off at the ground. You see that they'll be crossing your row within seconds at the rate they're moving.

"Run for the station!" you cry. Everyone looks surprised that you seem afraid of the harmless plant-eaters. "They're blind!" you explain. "They feed entirely by smell, and we've got mannakan juice on our legs! They'll mow us down, too!"

"Dru's right!" yells Seel. "There are too many to fight! We'll be eaten just like those plants!" The Dralasite begins to stretch his three legs as far as possible, taking longer steps each time. Behind him, you all race for

the white buildings of Station Alpha in the distance.

You are almost at the station when two humans in camouflage skeinsuits leap into your path, quickly setting up a large weapon on a tripod. It's a sonic devastator! At this range, the massive sound waves would tear you all to shreds in seconds!

"Get down!" yells Brim, drawing his gyrojet pistol. Suddenly the sound of laser fire is all around you! "There are too many of them!" Brim shouts. "Hold your fire!"

You hold your stunner high in the air, following Brim's example. A large number of humans and Yazirians surround you from all sides and seize your weapons roughly. They're all dressed in the same camouflage armor and have weapons bearing the black and red emblem of the Pan-Galactic Corporation!

They seem very interested in Kit. A dozen of the fighters surround the cybot, as if they expect Kit to attack at any second.

"Where did that cybot bug come from?" demands a tall thin man.

"It's mine!" Skitsi buzzes, edging his huge body forward. "I'm a chief scientist of the Corporation, and that cybot is my assistant!"

Before the tall man can reply, you jump in front of the Vrusk. "Where are my parents?" you demand. The officer studies your face with interest.

"I'll ask the questions here," he says calmly. "Who are you, and who are your parents?"

"My name is Andru Clayton," you tell him, "and I'm Ann and Mark Clayton's son. I grew up here at Station Alpha, and I demand to see my parents immediately!"

"The boy's telling the truth," Brim says to the officer. "I'm Brim Darkstar, commander of this team. We've been sent to New Pale by the Corporation to find out why the mannakan shipments have ceased."

The officer whispers something to one of the fighters, then turns back to you. "Follow me to the laboratory," he says. "If you're really the chief's son, I know someone who'll want to talk to you."

You start walking behind the tall human. Over your shoulder, you see that the others are being taken to one of the larger buildings. The officer leads you directly to the central building, which you recognize as your father's laboratory.

Please turn to page 97.

"I can't promise to keep quiet," you tell the Ranger. "I'm worried about my parents, and I want to help them. If that means going to someone outside of Star Law, I will!"

Captain Tyson rises abruptly. "In that case, Dru, we can't help you," he says. "I appreciate your honesty, though, and I'll try to let you know about your parents as soon as possible."

You're confused as you walk back to the Pan-Galactic Corporation. You decide to ask Dean Luxtar at the Computer Institute for advice. As an officer of the Corporation, like your parents, he may know something you can do.

The dean nods his heavy Vrusk's head with its polished black mandibles as he listens to your story. When you tell him about your visit to Star Law Headquarters, Luxtar's antennae twitch with interest.

"That's very curious, Dru," he buzzes. "Our friends in the Federation seem worried about New Pale, too. All I know is that some of our merchant ships have reported some unusual difficulties trying to land at the starport on your home planet. Let me call a few people I know who might be able to help."

You thank Dean Luxtar and go to your dormitory room. After some time, you fall asleep, worried and exhausted. You are awakened by the sound of someone calling your name. You sit up quickly, only to see a cybot standing by your bed, trying to awaken you!

Please turn to page 16.

"I can't disagree with Jan. The mission is more important than our safety," you tell Brim. "I think we should split up and finish the job we started."

Brim stares at your serious face for a moment, then smiles. "You're a courageous boy, Dru," he says with obvious respect. "Not many people could have made that decision."

"We can take this pile of plasteel with us," says Erl, pointing at Kit. "Skitsi programmed it with a map of the city. This bug can show us right to the Brain's back door!"

Brim nods his approval. "Good thinking, Erl. But what about Seel and the others? Dru, why don't you stay here as an extra gun in case the Brain finds them?"

You feel a rush of disappointment at Brim's suggestion. You want to go with Brim and Erl because your computer skills might be useful, but you're also worried about leaving Seel behind with two injured team members. You wish Darkstar would just order you to do one thing or the other.

"Dru, it's up to you," he says. "There'll be plenty of danger either way, so you needn't feel ashamed whatever you decide."

1) If you choose to stay behind with Jan, Seel, and Skitsi, turn to page 45.

2) If you decide to go on to the Brain Room with Brim, Erl, and Kit, turn to page 135.

"Wait, Erl!" you yell quickly. "Maybe I can reach the manual controls and stop it!"

The Yazirian lowers his laser pistol while you run for the side of the huge machine. Its photoeyes don't seem to notice you as it continues straight toward the scouter.

You see the metal ladder leading to the control cabin and grab the first rung. As you climb into the cabin, you see the others running for the scouter. One look at the control panel is enough to see that the harvester is set on automatic. That means that the giant agbot is locked into its computer control system. There's no way you can stop the heavy machine from crashing into the scouter!

Suddenly you see Ch'oth Erl and Darkstar step directly into the path of the rampaging robot. Erl aims his laser pistol at one tread while Darkstar points his gyrojet gun at the other. You see the blasts from the two weapons at the same time. The agbot shudders to a stop as the shots destroy the treads on both sides of the heavy robot. You can still hear the steady hum of the nuclear engine as it tries to turn the broken treads.

You are trying to cut the engine off when a red warning light starts to flash on the instrument panel. The nuclear power plant is overheating! If it melts, the harvester will explode, destroying you, the scouter, Unit Five, and Station Alpha in a matter of seconds!

Please turn to page 125.

"I've always gone into the Computer Center from the street," you say. "But I'm sure the Brain has that entrance guarded."

"What about the tunnel?" asks Jan.

"I remember something about an emergency escape route from the basement," you reply, "but I've never seen it."

"Let me look at that map," says Brim, then examines it intently. "It reminds me of the underground service system we used on Triad to escape from the Sathar's warbot."

"It should!" says Packy. "We followed the Triad plan when we designed it!"

"That's it, then!" says Brim. "The service tunnels on Triad are used as emergency escape routes, just as Dru remembers. Since the Computer Center has a top priority, all tunnels must connect with its basement!"

"But won't the Brain be watching the tunnel?" asks Seel.

"I doubt it," Brim says. "That tunnel is packed with high voltage cables, and it's patrolled constantly by garbots programmed to eat anything that doesn't belong there. That's the last place the Brain would guard!"

"Garbots, eh?" says Erl. "Those big vacuum cleaners aren't so tough! Let's go!"

Soon you are speeding toward Truane City in Station Alpha's only jetcopter.

"The tunnel makes a series of rings around the Computer Center, like a giant target with the computer building for a bull's-eye," says Brim. "The farthest ring extends to the edge of the first mannakan field. We shouldn't go any closer than that with the copter."

As you near the edge of the field, Brim cuts the jets and flies the copter like a regular chopper, hovering so low that the mannakan tassels brush the landing skids. The Unit Five commander lands the machine lightly on the field. Within minutes, everyone is running toward the tunnel entrance.

Erl is the first to find the shaft. When you join the Yazirian, he is standing by the mushroom-shaped entrance hatch. You see a control box on the outside of the door, with a row of colored buttons.

"It's a combination lock!" says Skitsi. "If we push the wrong buttons or try to blow it up, the Brain will know right where we are!"

"I know the code!" you exclaim. "All the service systems use the same one! It's based on the changing colors of tree leaves: green, red, orange, yellow, and brown, in that order!"

"If Dru's sure about the colors, we could easily get in without the Brain knowing it," Brim says. "But if the Brain has changed the code, we might as well let Jan blow it open with kaboomite because of the alarm. It all depends on how sure Dru is about the code!"

1) If you feel sure of the color code and want to try it, turn to page 56.

2) But if you decide to let Jan blow a hole in the shaft, then turn to page 99.

"Stop!" you shout, aiming your stunner at Mellon. "Back away from those switches!"

Mellon freezes and turns slowly toward you. His old man's face loses some of its wrinkles, and he seems to grow taller. He sneers as he reaches up to his face with one hand and tears away a rubberized mask, revealing thick space-blue hair above the evil features of a much younger man!

"Don't you see that even Unit Five is helpless against us?" he says in a strong voice. Brim and Erl step to your side, their weapons trained on the mysterious stranger. Suddenly Mellon lunges toward a round dial on the computer panel.

"Stop him!" yells Brim. You feel the stunner hum in your hand as its blast slams into Mellon.

Erl runs to the strange blue-haired figure's side and feels for a pulse. "He'll be out for at least twenty minutes," he grunts.

"Is that enough time for you to figure out what's wrong with this machine, Dru?" asks Brim.

You're already flipping through the pages of the thick programming manual, trying to understand the complicated Level Six language. "I'm doing my best," you tell Brim, "but this stuff seems just too advanced for me!"

"Perhaps I may be of some help, Master Dru." You look up from the book to see Kit's shining mandibles.

"I may be able to explain some of the more difficult parts," intones the cybot. "I have only a Level Five system, but I should be able to handle most of the terms."

"Go to it, Kit!" you exclaim, handing it the manual.

Kit's Vruskoid claws thumb through the book so fast that you can't even make out a word. In less than a minute, Kit hands you the book.

"It seems that you wish to restore the Brain to its original program," says the cybot.

"That's right," you reply. "But how can we do that? Is it possible?"

"Certainly!" says Kit. "Simply pick a date before the new instructions were given. Then tell the Brain to stop following all programs introduced after that date."

"Of course!" you shout. "But what date should we use? How do we know when the new program was fed into the computer?"

"Why don't you use the same date you left for school?" suggests Brim. "You know everything was normal then."

You let Kit show you the right buttons to push, then tell the Brain to cease to obey everything anyone told it to do since the day you left for Gran Quivera. The tiny lights flash on the control panel as the Brain processes your command. Suddenly the speaker on the wall starts to crackle, and you hear the sound of human voices.

"Hello! . . . Hello! Can anyone hear me?"

calls a woman's voice. It takes a moment for you to realize it's the voice of your mother!

"Mom! This is Dru! Can you hear me?"

"Dru!" she gasps. "Where are you, Son?"

"I'm in the central computer room, Mom," you reply. "Some friends and I have just deprogrammed the Brain!"

"You're just across the street from us!" your mother exclaims. "Son, whatever you did really worked! The cybots stopped guarding us and the cell doors opened automatically! We saw the cybodragons fold their wings and drop like stones to the pavement. Mark and I will be right over, Dru. Good work, son!"

"What'll we do with this blue-haired creep?" grunts Erl.

"There are still a lot of details we don't have," says Brim. "We need to take him back to Port Loren and turn him over to Star Law, but it might be wise to question him before we leave the planet. Then again, we might be able to get all the information we want from the Brain's memory before Mellon wakes up. What do you think, Dru?" he asks. "Can you get the details from the Brain, or should we question Mellon right away?"

1) If you want to search the Brain's memory before Mellon wakes up, turn to page 147.

2) But if you'd rather question Mellon, turn to page 155.

"Right!" agrees Brim. "There's no need to tell everyone down there we're landing."

"Can you block their radar?" you ask.

"Good thinking, Dru!" says Brim approvingly. "You're turning out to be quite a spaceman!" Jan switches on the force field to confuse the radar units at the starport.

As the scouter enters the highest clouds of New Pale's atmosphere, you feel the antigrav device slow the ship. You glance toward Brim and Jan, and it's obvious to you that the two adventurers are enjoying this rare opportunity to land a spacecraft without a computer.

"Look, Dru!" Jan calls. In the viewer, you see the familiar high plains, with their thick green forests and crystal lakes. The blue mannakan fields surround the plateaus, like a great ocean dotted with green islands.

"Now it's time for our resident expert on New Pale to suggest a landing site," Brim says seriously. "Shall we put down in one of those forests or in a mannakan field, Dru?"

"Or in Truane City, perhaps?" adds Jan.

1) If you decide to suggest landing in the forest, turn to page 131.

2) If you think it would be best to land in the mannakan fields, turn to page 84.

3) But if you want to recommend that the ship lands at Truane City, turn to page 31.

You leap from the cabin to the ladder and slide to the ground, yelling wildly.

"The reactor's overheating! Take cover!"

Jan races toward the crippled agbot. She leaps smoothly into the cabin, and for a minute of breathless fear, everyone watches as the beautiful demolitionist works on the wires of the control panel. Finally her bright smile appears at the window of the harvester.

"It's stopped!" she calls, just as the tread wheels stop spinning. Everyone runs to the stalled machine.

"Dru! I need your advice," calls Skitsi.

The Vrusk scientist is examining the agbot's computer. A steady beeping sound comes from the radio, while the video screen flashes a strange pattern of lines.

"This computer still seems to be working even though the power is off!" says Skitsi. "What do you know about these machines?"

"It's just a small Level Two computer," you answer. "It can be powered from the agbot's energy source or by remote control."

"Well, someone is trying to control it right now!" clicks Skitsi excitedly. "What do those flashing lines mean, Kit?"

The Vruskoid cybot studies the video screen for several seconds. "The operator is demanding to know why this robot has not destroyed itself and is telling it to do so immediately." You can't imagine how a message could have been contained in those strange lines.

"Can you identify the operator?" Brim asks.

"Only if I am plugged into the console," Kit answers. Skitsi orders his cybot twin to trace the mysterious operator of the agbot. Immediately Kit disconnects the receiver from the computer and plugs it in to his own voicebox.

Suddenly the cybot's photoeyes flash rapidly. "WHO ARE YOU?" demands a deep voice, using Kit's voicebox. "IDENTIFY YOURSELF!"

Kit seems to be in a trance as it responds to the strange voice. "I am a Series Ten, Level Five Vruskoid cybot, designated by my masters as 'Bi-Zkit,'" answers Kit.

"WHY ARE YOU INTERFERING WITH MY AGBOT? FEED ALL OF YOUR DATA TO ME IMMEDIATELY, BI-ZKIT!" intones the deep voice.

"Pull the plug!" Brim orders suddenly.

"Don't let them know who we are!"

"No!" clicks Skitsi. "Kit is programmed to hide its data. We'll find out who that voice is if we leave Kit connected!"

You are closer than anyone else to the cybot and could disconnect Kit almost instantly from the radio panel. But should you?

1) If you think you should follow Brim Darkstar's orders and unplug Kit from the radio panel, turn to page 63.

2) If you think you should follow Skitsi's advice and risk letting Kit identify the operator, turn to page 42.

"I just don't think Kit is strong enough to handle the Brain," you tell Brim. "Maybe Kit can use the map in its memory to help us figure out which door leads to the Brain."

"Go ahead and try it," Darkstar says.

You instruct Kit to study the map and to compute the size of a machine that could control all of the equipment in Truane City, plus the mannakan operations.

"Even with the smallest microcircuits, such a machine would measure at least ten thousand cubic meters," Kit replies matter-of-factly.

You look in surprise at Brim's face and see that he has reached the same conclusion.

"That's as large as this entire floor!" you exclaim. "We're inside the Brain right now!"

"What do you mean?" asks Erl.

"I've been in the programming room, but never anywhere else in the Computer Center," you explain to the confused Yazirian. "This must be a service corridor somewhere right in the middle of the Brain. Any one of these doors will lead to the programming room!"

"You lead the way, Dru," Brim orders.

The first door opens into a narrow hall between two rows of spotless silver cabinets.

"We're in the memory core," you tell Brim and Erl. "The control panel can't be far."

"Won't it know we're inside it?" whispers Erl, looking like a trapped monkey.

"I doubt it," you say. "A Level Six doesn't have any sensors on the inside. I guess that's why there was a terminal out in the corridor."

You start following the twisting passage through the maze of gleaming metal cabinets. After walking for some time, you turn a corner and stumble suddenly into the large programming room you remember!

The room is empty except for a wall of video screens and buttons. A small human, clad in the familiar blue coveralls of the Corporation, stands in front of the control panel holding a bulky programming manual in one hand and pressing buttons with the other.

A look of surprise covers his dry, shriveled face as you burst into the room with your weapons raised. You see a very old man with a fringe of long gray hair hanging around a shiny bald head. His face is so wrinkled that he reminds you of a mummy. Only his eyes appear young. You notice with a start that they're a strange, bright purple!

When he sees your weapons and the Corporation skeinsuits, he smiles, showing old yellowed teeth, and turns away from the panel.

"You may put your weapons away," he says softly. "I work for the Corporation, too." None of you relax your guns, however.

"Who are you?" Brim demands. "And what are you doing at that control panel?"

"Why, I'm programming the master computer, of course!" he exclaims, as if nothing unusual has been happening. "I am Senior Programmer Mellon. Until quite recently, I was held captive in the Security Center, along with every other scientist in Truane City. It seems that this unfortunate machine has developed some minor programming errors, which I am now trying to correct."

"How did you escape from the Security Building?" Brim demands.

"I'm really not sure," replies Mellon.

"Do you recognize this man?" Brim whispers to you.

"No," you reply, "but I wouldn't know any of the senior programmers. Let me ask him some questions." Holding your stunner on the man, you walk toward him. "Tell me, Mr. Mellon," you begin, "have you seen my parents, Ann and Mark Clayton?" The bright purple eyes study you carefully for a moment.

"You're Andru Clayton, the young computer wizard!" he exclaims. "Your parents are in good health, Andru, and will be free as soon as I finish with this new program. Come here, and bring that cybot with you! With your help, I can put an end to this craziness immediately!" Mellon turns back to the control board and reaches for a lever, but you must decide whether to trust this strange man.

1) If you decide to trust this strange old man and help him, turn to page 101.

2) If you decide not to trust the man and think you should prevent him from touching the control panel, turn to page 120.

"It might be dangerous to land in the city," you advise Darkstar. "If everything were safe there, the spaceport computer would still be working. As for the mannakan fields, I don't like the looks of them. They're usually full of robots at this time of day, and I don't see a single one moving around down there!"

"So you recommend we land in the forest?"

"Yes," you reply. "We can stay in the woods long enough to scout the fields. I know those forests like the back of my hand."

"That sounds logical," Skitsi buzzes, his antennae twitching impatiently. "Let's get on with it!"

Brim smiles and prepares to land the scouter while Erl and Seel head for the cargo hold to get the equipment ready. "Come over here, Dru," Brim orders, "and help me find a landing site."

You join Darkstar at his console. In the viewer, you see the vast fields of blue mannakan, dotted with great green islands of trees and lakes. Suddenly you see familiar buildings on the fringe of a large field.

"I know where we are!" you exclaim. "That's Station Alpha, where my father opened his first field laboratory! There's a perfect landing spot next to the lake!"

"Sounds like just the ticket!" says Brim. The veteran space explorer slows the scouter and drifts over the tops of the trees until you see the familiar lake where your father often took you fishing.

Jan points to an opening in the trees by the lake. Darkstar nods his approval, and she flicks on the antigrav.

The scouter floats softly to the surface of New Pale without incident. Erl and Seel hand out everyone's equipment, including your new skeinsuit armor and electrostunner pistol. In minutes, you are standing once more on your home planet with your new friends of Unit Five. You notice immediately that something seems strange, and it takes you several minutes to realize what it is.

"It's too quiet!" you whisper. "No squirds, no whistlies—not a sound!"

"A scouter is big enough to scare most wild creatures off," suggests Seel. Suddenly the Dralasite's sensitive skin begins to quiver.

"What is it, Seel?" Jan asks urgently.

"I smell something strange," he murmurs.

"What does it smell like?" asks Brim.

"Like a mixture of feathers and fur," Seel answers, "and a lot of them!"

You chuckle out loud, and everyone looks at you. "He smells squirds!" you exclaim. "We'll probably see them as soon as we get into those trees." Brim lets you lead the way to the edge of the forest, where you hear a sound like something between a chirp and a chatter.

Suddenly the trees are alive with hundreds of little creatures scurrying from limb to limb above your heads. The startled Yazirian, his sensitive eyes now covered by dark goggles, reflexively whips out his laser pistol.

"Don't, Erl!" you exclaim, grabbing his arm. "They're just birds, except with fur! We keep them for pets on New Pale."

You feel the Yazirian's arm relax. The squirds disappear deeper into the forest, leaving the woods as strangely quiet as before. Once more you have the feeling that something is terribly wrong.

"My father's lab is that way," you tell everyone, pointing to a small forest trail, "but something has changed."

"What do you think we should do, Dru?" asks Jan. "Should we head for Station Alpha?"

"I suggest we get back in the scouter and look at Station Alpha from the air," Skitsi buzzes quickly. "There's no need to take unnecessary chances."

"Why don't you and that plasteel twin of yours just go back to the ship and leave the risky stuff to us professionals?" snorts Erl.

"Quit squabbling!" Brim demands, turning to you. "It's your planet, Dru. What do you suggest?"

1) If you want to go straight through the forest to Station Alpha, turn to page 141.

2) If you think Skitsi's idea was a good one and want to return to the scouter to scout the station from the air, turn to page 153.

"I think it would be better for all of us if I helped you find the Brain," you tell Brim. "Jan and Seel can take care of themselves. Besides, I'm the best computer specialist you've got, now that Skitsi's out of action!"

Darkstar grins at your argument. "Check your gear, Dru. You're going with us!" he says with an approving smile.

You tell Jan and Seel a quick good-bye and follow Kit's fast-moving body across the archway toward the center of Truane City.

The corridor connecting the circular tunnels extends straight as an arrow into the heart of the city. It takes you less than an hour to reach the end, where you find yourself facing a round door panel with a panel lock just like the one on the mushroom shaft!

"What do we do now?" asks Erl, drawing his blaster.

"Put that down!" says Brim. "We'd have cybots all over us! Dru, do you think you learned anything from that panel lock outside?"

"I think I may have switched the order of the red and orange buttons," you say. "It might work if I press the orange one first, but I'm not sure."

"It's our best chance!" says Brim. "If it doesn't work, Erl can blast it and we'll take our chances!"

You take a deep breath and step up to the panel. Then you press the buttons rapidly, making sure to press orange before red. You are prepared to hear the alarm, but instead the circular door simply slides open like the lens of a camera!

The four of you dash through the hatch, which closes silently behind you. You find yourselves in a large circular room, with dials, gauges, and control boxes covering the walls. There are also more of the round, computer-locked hatches leading from other central corridors. In the center of the room, you spot an elevator shaft with the doors open and a car waiting.

"Where are we, Kit?" you ask the cybot.

"At this point, we are at the very center of Truane City," Kit reports, "in the basement of the Computer Center."

"Can you tell us where to find the Brain?" Brim asks the cybot.

"According to the map data, the central computer is located on the eighth floor of this building," Kit replies unemotionally.

"That's good enough for me!" says Erl. With a swirl of his scarlet cloak, the hairy Yazirian races for the elevator. For once, you don't need to get past a panel lock. All you have to do is press the button marked "8."

Please turn to page 33.

"I don't think we'd learn anything at Station Alpha," you say. "It looked deserted when we flew over it. Besides, that voice must be connected somehow with the main computer at Truane City."

Brim nods. "Truane City it is. Let's take the scouter. We'll save a lot of time that way, and we won't need to worry about another runaway agbot!"

"Or worse!" adds Seel.

"You just stay with me," Erl tells the nervous Dralasite. "We won't let anything happen to our favorite little blob!"

In minutes, you're all safely inside the scouter and headed for Truane City, New Pale's only spaceport. You see the towers of Truane city far below.

"See if anything is moving down there, Skitsi," orders Brim. The Vrusk scientist scans the city with a seismometer, a machine that you know can detect the movement of a man on a planet's surface from a low space orbit!

After several minutes, Skitsi clicks his black mandibles. "Nothing!" he buzzes. "I've never seen anything like it! There's not even a maintenance robot moving down there. The whole city's dead!"

"Dru, where's the starport?" Brim demands. You study the viewer and soon see the round dome of the terminal.

"Straight ahead!" you reply. "It's that round building. I can see two or three shuttles still on the ground."

"I see them, too!" says Jan. "They look like Corporation shuttles." You soon recognize them as mannakan shipments that never left New Pale!

"Brim, those shuttles were stopped before they could take off!" you exclaim. "That means someone let more than three hundred tons of mannakan spoil on the ground!"

"Three hundred tons!" gasps Erl. "That's probably worth more than half a million credits!"

"Easily," Brim says, "and much more now that it's scarce! Whoever's behind all of this doesn't seem to be interested in money! I'm setting us down!"

You start to check your equipment as Brim and Jan control the antigrav device, letting the scouter float downward until it is almost to the ground. Suddenly a glaring light almost blinds you, and a split second later the scouter jerks violently!

"What was THAT?" yells Erl.

"Lasers! Big ones!" answers Skitsi, his gray skin quivering nervously.

"Take us up, Jan!" Brim orders.

"I can't!" she shouts as smoke starts to fill the bridge. "We've taken a direct hit!"

Suddenly you see a huge machine rolling onto the concrete outside the terminal below you. It's the size of a small building and is surrounded by a shimmering halo of silver light.

"It's a warbot!" shouts Erl. "With an albedo screen!"

You know that lasers can't even scratch albedo screens. The scouter's laser cannons are useless against the warbot! You feel another powerful blast rock the small starship, and the scouter drops like a stone, crashing to the concrete right in front of the formidable war machine!

"Everybody out!" yells Brim.

You're lucky the scouter was so low. The fall only knocked you to the floor, and you scramble toward the hatch. But before you can reach it, the warbot's laser cannons fire their final deadly blast, bringing you and Unit Five to a fiery . . .

END

"The quickest way to reach Station Alpha is through the forest," you tell the others. "There's a trail just a few hundred meters from here that leads right to my dad's lab."

"Well, why're we standing here?" Erl demands gruffly. "Let's get going!"

"You scout ahead for the trail, Erl," says Brim. The heavily armed Yazirian trots on hairy, padded feet toward the forest, then looks back over his shoulder, sunlight flashing on his dark goggles. "Just follow my tracks!" he yells.

"Ch'oth Erl is a little hyperactive," says Seel in a soft, bubbling tone. He has sprouted two extra legs, for a total of five, and is doing his best to keep up with everyone.

"That's putting it mildly!" laughs Jan.

"He may be a bit impatient," says Brim, "but there's nobody I'd rather have on my side in a brawl. I've never met a better fighter! I once saw Erl handle four armed Yazirian assassins with just his sonic sword. He's a real martial artist!"

By the time you reach the trail to Station Alpha, Skitsi and Kit are already there waiting, thanks to their eight legs. Soon Seel catches up and you begin looking for Erl's tracks.

"There's one!" says Brim, pointing to an apelike footprint. Just then, a loud whistling howl pierces the forest ahead of you!

"What was that?" asks Jan.

"A whistlie!" you murmur. "Whistlies are

furry toadlike creatures. They're like alarm systems in the forests on New Pale. I'll bet Erl stepped on one!"

Within seconds, the dark forest is filled with the echoing howls of whistlies. Ch'oth Erl reappears and meets you with a disgusted look on his fierce muzzle.

"We'll never sneak up on anybody with all that going on! How do we shut off that racket?"

"I know a way. My father taught me a hunter's trick that works sometimes," you tell the Yazirian warrior, "but the rest of you better stay behind or we'll never get them quiet again!"

"Try it, Dru," says Brim. You nod and start down the trail. Erl walks by your side, searching the trees for a sign of the strange creatures.

"They won't be up there," you whisper. "Look on the ground, beside the trail." The high-pitched whistle has become almost more than you can stand when you finally spot one of them.

It rests in the shadows of a large bush, hidden by the changing patches of colors on its furry body. Its lipless mouth is round, and you see its throat moving in and out as it howls. You squat on the ground in front of it without moving a muscle, remembering your father's words: "Whistlies are almost blind and stone-deaf. They're frightened only by something large and moving. If you keep still long

enough, a frightened whistlie may relax and stop howling. Then, if you're still lucky, it'll move along so you can pass by."

The old hunter's trick works! The howls stop as quickly as they started. The whistlie first moves its owl-like head, then waddles off, its furry coat blending with every shadow it passes.

"Do you mean that all that racket came from one of those little things?" Erl asks.

"One was enough, wasn't it?" you reply. "Let's go back and get the others."

You start to follow the trail back to Brim and the rest of his crew. After only a few steps, you hear the crashing sound of heavy bodies landing on the trail behind you!

Erl's fighter's reflexes cause him to wheel around, his laser pistol raised to fire at the unknown attackers. Three shadowy figures in mottled forest colors have jumped from some low branches onto the trail behind you!

1) If you think you should fire your stunner at the attackers, turn to page 151.

2) If you decide to hold your fire, turn to page 92.

"I'm just not sure enough about my data to let the computer use it for an automatic landing," you decide. "Something strange is happening on New Pale, and it might interfere with our landing program."

"I disagree!" buzzes Skitsi from his computer console. "I wrote that program myself, and beyond a doubt, it's the safest way to land!"

"Don't pay any attention to that brainy bug, Brim," says Erl, glancing fiercely at the Vrusk. "He'd rather use a machine for everything!"

"I am responsible to the Corporation for the safety of this ship and its crew, Ch'oth Erl!" Skitsi clicks, chopping the air with his mandibles. "Our mission is always more important than your primitive urge for excitement!"

"Stop it, both of you!" Brim commands. "We'll do what Dru suggests and land this ship manually!"

"I advise total radio silence, and that includes any communication with the landing officer at Truane City," says Jan.

Please turn to page 124.

Remembering how powerful a runaway agbot can be, you draw your stunner.

"Shoot the treads!" you shout. "It's the only way we can stop it!"

Ch'oth Erl and Darkstar run to your side, their laser and gyrojet weapons drawn. As the heavy machine thunders toward you, all three weapons begin blasting at the tanklike treads.

You hear an earsplitting noise as the metal tracks snap and the agbot rumbles to a halt, its nuclear engine still humming. You leap for the ladder and pull yourself into the cabin.

You see immediately that the main switch is set on automatic. You try to turn it to the manual setting, but the switch won't budge! It's locked on computer control!

Just then, you notice a red warning light begin to flash on the instrument panel. The nuclear reactor that powers the engine is beginning to overheat! If it melts, the explosion will level Station Alpha and everything within twenty kilometers!

1) If you want to try to unlock the main switch with your robcomkit, turn to page 83.

2) If you decide instead to get away from the agbot and warn the others, turn to page 125.

"I think we should ask the Brain about Mellon," you tell Brim. "That way, we'd have at least some of the truth before we start to question him." You call Kit and ask the cybot to help you.

"Of course, Master Dru," it says quickly. "All you have to do is use the printer. The Brain will print everything Mellon placed in its memory since you left the planet."

In a matter of minutes, you have a complete printout, just as Kit said. As you read it, you are shaken by its terrible message. When you've finished, you hand the folded sheets to Brim without a word. The veteran explorer studies the printout grimly.

"Sathar!" he mutters, clenching his fist.

"What did you say, Brim?" demands Erl, a fierce sneer on his hairy lips. "Did you say 'Sathar'?"

"Mellon's a Sathar agent, Erl," you say softly, knowing that the mysterious wormlike creatures are the Yazirian's sworn life enemies. "He was instructed to destroy the mannakan fields by the Sathar, and he almost got away with it."

"There's more to it than just the mannakan," adds Brim. "For some reason, the Sathar want to stop any expansion of the Frontier toward Zebulon, and New Pale is right on the new starship route through the Xagyg dust clouds to the Zebulon system. The question is, why are the Sathar so interested in Zebulon?"

Erl is staring in fury at Mellon's body as the Sathar agent begins to stir. Before you or Brim can stop him, Erl has Mellon's shoulders in his powerful grasp.

"Talk! I said TALK, you miserable worm-lover!" screams the enraged Yazirian. "We know about your Sathar friends!"

Mellon's purple eyes widen with surprise when Erl mentions the sinister worm-people. Suddenly the man's whole body grows rigid. It trembles violently, then goes limp in Erl's arms. You see a broken plastic tooth roll from Mellon's mouth to the floor, emptied of its suicide pill.

"Poison!" exclaims Darkstar. "We won't get any more information from him!"

"But we do have the record!" you add. Brim looks at you and smiles.

"That's right, Dru," he says, "and we must get it to the Corporation as soon as possible. It looks as if our solution to one mystery has led us to one even more serious!"

Brim's mention of the Corporation is a sad reminder to you that your adventure with Unit Five has ended. You must return to the Computer Institute and complete your training. You're glad that the mission was successful, but you'll miss everyone in Unit Five.

"Brim, I'm—I'm glad you took me along as a guide," you say to the famous adventurer. "I'll never forget this past week!"

Brim looks at your serious face and frowns. "What do you mean?" he demands. "You've been far more than a guide on this mission! In fact, we might well have failed without you!"

"Brim's right," says Erl, with a grin on his hairy muzzle and a gleam in his goggled eyes. "If you hadn't been along, I would've had to listen to that big bug most of the time. Skitsi's a good scientist, but he's hardly the galaxy's most interesting conversationalist!"

"Dru, that reminds me of something," says Brim. "Skitsi's going to be out of action for a while, and we'll need somebody to help us with Kit and his other computer equipment. Do you think you could delay returning to the institute for a short time? I'd like to follow up on that idea about the Sathar and the Zebulon system as long as we're at this end of the galaxy. How about taking a short ride with us through the Xagyg dust clouds?"

Your smile is the only answer Brim needs to his wonderful suggestion. Another adventure seems headed your way after all. . . .

THE END

The three shadowy figures have barely landed on the ground when Erl fires his laser pistol. You draw your stunner and fire at the closest attacker. Two of the dark figures fall, and you swing your weapon toward a third. Suddenly you hear a small explosion behind you, and the last thing you remember is the thick cloud from a doze grenade enveloping you.

When you awake, you're lying on a cot of some kind, with your hands and feet tied to the rails. The room seems familiar, but you can't remember where you've seen it. Suddenly it pops into your groggy brain. This room is at Station Alpha!

Just then, the door slides open and two humans dressed in camouflage skeinsuits enter. One is a tall, thin man with a laser pistol, and the other is bulky and muscular, with a bushy black moustache.

"Where are my parents?" you demand as soon as they enter. "And where are my friends?"

"Just who are your parents, boy?" asks the heavy man with the moustache.

"I'm Andru Clayton! My parents built this research station! I was born here!"

The bulky man blinks. Then he motions for the tall one to follow him outside. You hear them mumbling excitedly in the hall as they walk away quickly. In a little while, you hear the sound of hurrying boots just before the door slides open. Another man rushes in, followed by the stout one. The newcomer is older, with silver streaks in his reddish hair and beard. As soon as he sees you, his tired brown eyes become moist with tears.

"Dru!" he cries. "How did you get here?" It's Pak Son-Til, your father's chief assistant! You've never seen him with a beard, and the combat clothes make him seem even stranger.

While the man with the moustache removes your ropes, you tell Packy everything that has happened. He sends the heavy man to see about your friends while you continue to shake off the effects of the doze grenade.

"What's going on, Packy?" you ask your old friend. "Where are my parents, anyway?"

Packy smiles sadly as you rub your wrists and ankles. "Let's go to the library, Dru," he says. "Your friends are waiting for us, and I need to tell them all about it, too!"

As the door to the library slides open, you see the rest of the Unit Five crew at a large table, studying a map. Skitsi and Kit are too busy with the map to pay much attention to you, but then, Vrusks are never very friendly.

Everyone else welcomes you warmly. "Enjoy your nap?" quips Erl as he hands you your stunner. You start to reply but decide to wait. Packy is at the head of the table, waiting for the commotion to die down. Your old friend is ready to reveal the secrets of the mysterious events on New Pale.

Please turn to page 105.

"I can't figure out exactly what's wrong with this place, but it's changed somehow," you tell Darkstar. "Just to be safe, I think we should take Skitsi's advice and fly over Station Alpha in the scouter."

"Bah!" says Erl. "We can handle anything in these woods! I thought you were brave!"

"Dru IS being brave, Ch'oth Erl!" Jan exclaims angrily. "Being careful isn't being cowardly! Leave him alone!"

"You human females are all alike!" Erl growls. "You and that bug would never take chances if Brim and I didn't make you!"

"Cool off, Erl!" orders Darkstar. "You know that Jan's as brave as anyone, including any Yazirian warrior! Or have you forgotten how she saved us all from that Sathar bomb on Minotaur? Would you try to disarm an alien bomb without tools or armor like she did?"

"All right!" says the gruff fighter. "We'll do it your way!" With a toss of his scarlet cape, he whirls around and stalks toward the scouter.

Jan smiles strangely at Brim Darkstar. "Brim, you really do surprise me sometimes!" she says, her dark eyes flashing.

You notice Brim's space-tanned face become even redder as he mumbles something about women and heads for the scouter. Jan winks at you and Seel, then you follow her into the ship.

The scouter's antigrav lifts you into the air in seconds. Soon you see the tops of trees in the viewer. There is no sign of anything moving, either in the fields or in the forest.

"Now, Dru," Brim says, "help me decide on a better place to land."

1) If you want to land near Station Alpha in the mannakan fields, turn to page 84.

2) If you would rather go to Truane City and land there, turn to page 31.

You advise Brim to question Mellon before doing anything else. The Brain's memory would always be there, but Mellon might not!

"We'll question him right now," says Brim, pulling a field hypo of stimdose from his belt pouch. The explorer injects the drug into Mellon's arm, and the man begins to stir immediately. As soon as the strange purple eyes open, you bend over his head.

"Your plot has failed, Mellon!" you tell him. "The Brain is back to normal. Make it easier on yourself and tell us why you did it."

A strange expression clouds Mellon's face. With a desperate cry, he slams his fist into your head and leaps to his feet, holding your stunner in his hand!

To your amazement, instead of firing at one of you, Mellon whirls around and fires a full blast at the main control panel! Sparks and smoke fill the room until the machine's automatic fire extinguishers begin to get it under control.

Erl's battle reflexes take over immediately. The Yazirian lunges forward and cracks Mellon on the head with the butt of his laser pistol. The strange man drops to his knees as your stunner falls to the floor.

"The program's gone forever!" Mellon whispers weakly. "You'll never find out why they wanted me to . . ." His words die on his lips as his body crashes to the floor.

"Mellon! Who are 'they'?" Brim shouts, but his eyes just stare blankly at the ceiling.

"Why did you hit him so hard?" you ask Erl. "Now we'll never know the true story!"

"It wasn't Erl who killed him," says Brim. "He killed himself with a poison capsule concealed inside this plastic tooth." You see the crushed tooth in Brim's tanned hand—the mark of a secret agent who failed his mission!

"Listen, Dru," says Darkstar seriously. "We may never know the full story about New Pale, but our mission was a success, thanks to you! The Frontier's filled with mysteries and adventures like this one, and we could use your help again. We'll keep a place in Unit Five open for you until you finish at the institute."

You can hardly believe your ears. You, a member of tho famous Unit Five team! Brim Darkstar's offer is the most exciting opportunity you've ever had, but you'll always wonder about the secret behind why these evil forces gathered on the fields of New Pale.

THE END

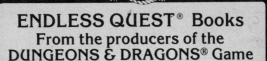

ENDLESS QUEST® Books
From the producers of the
DUNGEONS & DRAGONS® Game

For a free catalog, write
TSR, Inc.
P.O. Box 756, Dept. EQB
Lake Geneva, WI 53147

HEART QUEST™ BOOK

Pick a Path to Romance and Adventure™

**Now! From the producers of
ENDLESS QUEST® Books**

**It's your first romance,
and YOU must make the decisions!**

HEARTQUEST, ENDLESS QUEST, and PICK A PATH TO
ROMANCE AND ADVENTURE are trademarks owned by
TSR, Inc.
© 1983 by TSR, Inc.

For a free catalog, write:
  TSR, Inc.
  P.O. Box 756, Dept. HQB
  Lake Geneva, WI 53147

TSR, Inc.

The Official Fuel for Over 100,000 of the World's Most Imaginative Gamers

● DRAGON™ Magazine is a storehouse of information.

It's the acknowledged leader. No other hobby gaming magazine has the size and circulation.

● DRAGON™ Magazine is actually a monthly role-playing aid.

It fuels the best players with ammunition from the best writers. Imaginative articles by the co-creator of DUNGEONS & DRAGONS® games, E. Gary Gygax, appear in each issue. Hundreds of authors and games from all manufacturers are featured throughout. And with a cost of only $24 for your year's supply of fuel, it's hard to imagine how you got anywhere without it!

For information write:
Subscription Department, Dragon Publishing
Box 110, C186EQB Lake Geneva, WI 53147

DRAGON™ Magazine
Box 110, C186EQB'
Lake Geneva, WI 53147

In the UK:
TSR Hobbies,(UK)Ltd.
The Mill, Rathmore Rd.
Cambridge, ENGLAND
CB1 4AD

TSR Hobbies, Inc.
Products Of Your Imagination™